Dr. Jekyll and Mr. Hyde by Robert Louis Stevenson

With an afterword by
Jerome Charyn

T3-BHM-202

BANTAM BOOKS

TORONTO · NEW YORK · LONDON · SYDNEY · AUCKLAND

DR. JEKYLL AND MR. HYDE
A Bantam Book

PRINTING HISTORY
Dr. Jekyll and Mr. Hyde *was first published in 1886*
Bantam Classic edition / October 1981

2nd printing . . . February 1982   4th printing . . . . . March 1984
3rd printing . . . . February 1983   5th printing . . . . July 1985

*Cover painting, "View of Heath Street by
Night," (detail) by John Atkinson
Grimshaw. Courtesy of the Tate Gallery,
London.*

ISBN 0-553-21200-1

Published simultaneously in the United States and Canada

---

*Bantam Books are published by Bantam Books, Inc. Its trademark,
consisting of the words "Bantam Books" and the portrayal of a
rooster, is Registered in U.S. Patent and Trademark Office and
in other countries. Marca Registrada. Bantam Books, Inc., 666
Fifth Avenue, New York, New York 10103.*

PRINTED IN THE UNITED STATES OF AMERICA

O   14 13 12 11 10 9 8 7 6

Robert Louis Stevenson

Throughout his life, Robert Louis Stevenson was tormented by poor health. Yet despite frequent physical collapses—mainly due to constant respiratory illness—he was an indefatigable writer of novels, poems, essays, letters, travel books, and children's books. He was born on November 13, 1850, in Edinburgh, of a prosperous family of lighthouse engineers. Though he was expected to enter the family profession, he studied instead for the Scottish bar. By the time he was called to the bar, however, he had already begun writing seriously, and he never actually practiced law. In 1880, against his family's wishes, he married an American divorcée, Fanny Vandegrift Osbourne, who was ten years his senior; but the family was soon reconciled to the match, and the marriage proved a happy one.

All his life Stevenson traveled—often in a desperate quest for health. He and Fanny, having married in California and spent their honeymoon by an abandoned silver mine, traveled back to Scotland, then to Switzerland, to the south of France, to the American Adirondacks, and finally to the South Seas. As a novelist he was intrigued with the genius of place: *Treasure Island* (1883) began as a map to amuse a boy. Indeed, all his works reveal a profound sense of landscape and atmosphere: *Kidnapped* (1886); *The Strange Case of Dr. Jekyll and Mr. Hyde* (1886); *The Master of Ballantrae* (1889).

In 1889 Stevenson's deteriorating health exiled him to the tropics, and he settled in Samoa, where he was given patriarchal status by the natives. His health improved, yet he remained homesick for Scotland and it was to the "cold old huddle of grey hills" of the Lowlands that he returned in his last, unfinished masterpiece, *Weir of Hermiston* (1896).

Stevenson died suddenly on December 3, 1894, not of the long-feared tuberculosis, but of a cerebral hemorrhage. The kindly author of *Jekyll and Hyde* went down to the cellar to fetch a bottle of his favorite burgundy, uncorked it in the kitchen, abruptly cried out to his wife, "what's the matter with me, what is this strangeness, *has my face changed*?"—and fell to the floor. The brilliant storyteller and master of transformations had been struck down at forty-four, at the height of his creative powers.

Bantam Classics
Ask your bookseller for these other British Classics

BEOWULF AND OTHER OLD ENGLISH POEMS
   Translated by Constance B. Hieatt
THE CANTERBURY TALES by Geoffrey Chaucer
ROBINSON CRUSOE by Daniel Defoe
GULLIVER'S TRAVELS AND OTHER WRITINGS by Jonathan Swift
PRIDE AND PREJUDICE by Jane Austen
EMMA by Jane Austen
SENSE AND SENSIBILITY by Jane Austen
MANSFIELD PARK by Jane Austen
PERSUASION by Jane Austen
FRANKENSTEIN by Mary Shelley
JANE EYRE by Charlotte Brontë
WUTHERING HEIGHTS by Emily Brontë
DAVID COPPERFIELD by Charles Dickens
GREAT EXPECTATIONS by Charles Dickens
HARD TIMES by Charles Dickens
OLIVER TWIST by Charles Dickens
A TALE OF TWO CITIES by Charles Dickens
NICHOLAS NICKLEBY by Charles Dickens
BLEAK HOUSE by Charles Dickens
THE PICKWICK PAPERS by Charles Dickens
A CHRISTMAS CAROL by Charles Dickens
BARCHESTER TOWERS and THE WARDEN by Anthony Trollope
SILAS MARNER by George Eliot
MIDDLEMARCH by George Eliot
FAR FROM THE MADDING CROWD by Thomas Hardy
TESS OF THE D'URBERVILLES by Thomas Hardy
JUDE THE OBSCURE by Thomas Hardy
THE MAYOR OF CASTERBRIDGE by Thomas Hardy
THE RETURN OF THE NATIVE by Thomas Hardy
CHANCE by Joseph Conrad
HEART OF DARKNESS and THE SECRET SHARER
   by Joseph Conrad
LORD JIM by Joseph Conrad
THE SECRET AGENT by Joseph Conrad
DR. JEKYLL AND MR. HYDE by Robert Louis Stevenson
TREASURE ISLAND by Robert Louis Stevenson
KIDNAPPED by Robert Louis Stevenson
DRACULA by Bram Stoker
CAPTAINS COURAGEOUS by Rudyard Kipling
KIM by Rudyard Kipling
ALICE'S ADVENTURES IN WONDERLAND and THROUGH THE
   LOOKING-GLASS by Lewis Carroll
THE MOONSTONE by Wilkie Collins
THE WOMAN IN WHITE by Wilkie Collins
THE PICTURE OF DORIAN GRAY AND OTHER WRITINGS
   by Oscar Wilde
THE TIME MACHINE by H. G. Wells
THE INVISIBLE MAN by H. G. Wells
THE WIND IN THE WILLOWS by Kenneth Grahame
PETER PAN by J. M. Barrie
LADY CHATTERLEY'S LOVER by D. H. Lawrence

Dr. Jekyll
and Mr. Hyde

Story of the Door

MR. UTTERSON the lawyer was a man of a rugged countenance that was never lighted by a smile; cold, scanty and embarrassed in discourse; backward in sentiment; lean, long, dusty, dreary and yet somehow lovable. At friendly meetings, and when the wine was to his taste, something eminently human beaconed from his eye; something indeed which never found its way into his talk, but which spoke not only in these silent symbols of the after-dinner face, but more often and loudly in the acts of his life. He was austere with himself; drank gin when he was alone, to mortify a taste for vintages; and though he enjoyed the theater, had not crossed the doors of one for twenty years. But he had an approved tolerance for others; sometimes wondering, almost with envy, at the high pressure of spirits involved in their misdeeds; and in any extremity inclined to help rather than to reprove. "I incline to Cain's heresy," he used to say quaintly: "I let my brother go to the devil in his own way." In this character, it was frequently his fortune to be the last reputable acquaintance and the last good influence in the lives of downgoing men. And to such as these, so long as they came about his

chambers, he never marked a shade of change in
his demeanour.

No doubt the feat was easy to Mr. Utterson; for
he was undemonstrative at the best, and even his
friendship seemed to be founded in a similar catho-
licity of good-nature. It is the mark of a modest
man to accept his friendly circle ready-made from
the hands of opportunity; and that was the lawyer's way. His friends were those of his own blood
or those whom he had known the longest; his af-
fections, like ivy, were the growth of time, they im-
plied no aptness in the object. Hence, no doubt,
the bond that united him to Mr. Richard Enfield,
his distant kinsman, the well-known man about
town. It was a nut to crack for many, what these
two could see in each other, or what subject they
could find in common. It was reported by those
who encountered them in their Sunday walks, that
they said nothing, looked singularly dull, and
would hail with obvious relief the appearance of a
friend. For all that, the two men put the greatest
store by these excursions, counted them the chief
jewel of each week, and not only set aside occa-
sions of pleasure, but even resisted the calls of
business, that they might enjoy them uninterrupted.

It chanced on one of these rambles that their
way led them down a by-street in a busy quarter of
London. The street was small and what is called
quiet, but it drove a thriving trade on the week-
days. The inhabitants were all doing well, it seemed,
and all emulously hoping to do better still, and

laying out the surplus of their grains in coquetry; so that the shop fronts stood along that thoroughfare with an air of invitation, like rows of smiling saleswomen. Even on Sunday, when it veiled its more florid charms and lay comparatively empty of passage, the street shone out in contrast to its dingy neighbourhood, like a fire in a forest; and with its freshly painted shutters, well-polished brasses, and general cleanliness and gaiety of note, instantly caught and pleased the eye of the passenger.

Two doors from one corner, on the left hand going east, the line was broken by the entry of a court; and just at that point, a certain sinister block of building thrust forward its gable on the street. It was two storeys high; showed no window, nothing but a door on the lower storey and a blind forehead of discoloured wall on the upper; and bore in every feature, the marks of prolonged and sordid negligence. The door, which was equipped with neither bell nor knocker, was blistered and distained. Tramps slouched into the recess and struck matches on the panels; children kept shop upon the steps; the schoolboy had tried his knife on the mouldings; and for close on a generation, no one had appeared to drive away these random visitors or to repair their ravages.

Mr. Enfield and the lawyer were on the other side of the by-street; but when they came abreast of the entry, the former lifted up his cane and pointed.

"Did you ever remark that door?" he asked; and

when his companion had replied in the affirmative,
"It is connnected in my mind," added he, "with
a very odd story."

"Indeed?" said Mr. Utterson, with a slight change
of voice, "and what was that?"

"Well, it was this way," returned Mr. Enfield:
"I was coming home from some place at the end of
the world, about three o'clock of a black winter
morning, and my way lay through a part of town
where there was literally nothing to be seen but
lamps. Street after street, and all the folks asleep
—street after street, all lighted up as if for a procession and all as empty as a church—till at last I got
into that state of mind when a man listens and listens and begins to long for the sight of a policeman. All at once, I saw two figures: one a little
man who was stumping along eastward at a good
walk, and the other a girl of maybe eight or ten
who was running as hard as she was able down a
cross street. Well, sir, the two ran into one another
naturally enough at the corner; and then came
the horrible part of the thing; for the man trampled
calmly over the child's body and left her screaming on the ground. It sounds nothing to hear, but it
was hellish to see. It wasn't like a man; it was like
some damned Juggernaut. I gave a view halloa,
took to my heels, collared my gentleman, and
brought him back to where there was already quite
a group about the screaming child. He was perfectly cool and made no resistance, but gave me
one look, so ugly that it brought out the sweat on

me like running. The people who had turned out were the girl's own family; and pretty soon, the doctor, for whom she had been sent, put in his appearance. Well, the child was not much the worse, more frightened, according to the Sawbones; and there you might have supposed would be an end to it. But there was one curious circumstance. I had taken a loathing to my gentleman at first sight. So had the child's family, which was only natural. But the doctor's case was what struck me. He was the usual cut and dry apothecary, of no particular age and colour, with a strong Edinburgh accent, and about as emotional as a bagpipe. Well, sir, he was like the rest of us; every time he looked at my prisoner, I saw that Sawbones turn sick and white with desire to kill him. I knew what was in his mind, just as he knew what was in mine; and killing being out of the question, we did the next best. We told the man we could and would make such a scandal out of this, as should make his name stink from one end of London to the other. If he had any friends or any credit, we undertook that he should lose them. And all the time, as we were pitching it in red hot, we were keeping the women off him as best we could, for they were as wild as harpies. I never saw a circle of such hateful faces; and there was the man in the middle, with a kind of black, sneering coolness—frightened too, I could see that—but carrying it off, sir, really like Satan. 'If you choose to make capital out of this accident,'

said he, 'I am naturally helpless. No gentleman but
wishes to avoid a scene,' says he. 'Name your figure.' Well, we screwed him up to a hundred pounds
for the child's family; he would have clearly liked
to stick out; but there was something about the lot
of us that meant mischief, and at last he struck.
The next thing was to get the money; and where
do you think he carried us but to that place with
the door?—whipped out a key, went in, and presently came back with the matter of ten pounds in
gold and a cheque for the balance on Coutts's,
drawn payable to bearer and signed with a name
that I can't mention, though it's one of the points
of my story, but it was a name at least very well
known and often printed. The figure was stiff;
but the signature was good for more than that, if
it was only genuine. I took the liberty of pointing
out to my gentleman that the whole business
looked apocryphal, and that a man does not, in
real life, walk into a cellar door at four in the
morning and come out with another man's cheque
for close upon a hundred pounds. But he was quite
easy and sneering. 'Set your mind at rest,' says he,
'I will stay with you till the banks open and cash
the cheque myself.' So we all set off, the doctor,
and the child's father, and our friend and myself,
and passed the rest of the night in my chambers;
and next day, when we had breakfasted, went in a
body to the bank. I gave in the cheque myself, and
said I had every reason to believe it was a forgery.
Not a bit of it. The cheque was genuine."

"Tut-tut," said Mr. Utterson.

"I see you feel as I do," said Mr. Enfield. "Yes, it's a bad story. For my man was a fellow that nobody could have to do with, a really damnable man; and the person that drew the cheque is the very pink of the proprieties, celebrated too, and (what makes it worse) one of your fellows who do what they call good. Black mail, I suppose; an honest man paying through the nose for some of the capers of his youth. Black Mail House is what I call the place with the door, in consequence. Though even that, you know, is far from explaining all," he added, and with the words fell into a vein of musing.

From this he was recalled by Mr. Utterson asking rather suddenly: "And you don't know if the drawer of the cheque lives there?"

"A likely place, isn't it?" returned Mr. Enfield. "But I happen to have noticed his address; he lives in some square or other."

"And you never asked about the—place with the door?" said Mr. Utterson.

"No, sir: I had a delicacy," was the reply. "I feel very strongly about putting questions; it partakes too much of the style of the day of judgment. You start a question, and it's like starting a stone. You sit quietly on the top of a hill; and away the stone goes, starting others; and presently some bland old bird (the last you would have thought of) is knocked on the head in his own back garden and the family have to change their name. No sir, I make

it a rule of mine: the more it looks like Queer
Street, the less I ask."

"A very good rule, too," said the lawyer.

"But I have studied the place for myself," continued Mr. Enfield. "It seems scarcely a house.
There is no other door, and nobody goes in or out
of that one but, once in a great while, the gentleman of my adventure. There are three windows
looking on the court on the first floor; none below;
the windows are always shut but they're clean. And
then there is a chimney which is generally smok-
ing; so somebody must live there. And yet it's not
so sure; for the buildings are so packed together
about the court, that it's hard to say where one
ends and another begins."

The pair walked on again for a while in silence;
and then "Enfield," said Mr. Utterson, "that's a
good rule of yours."

"Yes, I think it is," returned Enfield.

"But for all that," continued the lawyer, "there's
one point I want to ask: I want to ask the name
of that man who walked over the child."

"Well," said Mr. Enfield, "I can't see what harm
it would do. It was a man of the name of Hyde."

"Hm," said Mr. Utterson. "What sort of a man is
he to see?"

"He is not easy to describe. There is something
wrong with his appearance; something displeasing,
something down-right detestable. I never saw a
man I so disliked, and yet I scarce know why. He
must be deformed somewhere; he gives a strong

feeling of deformity, although I couldn't specify the point. He's an extraordinary looking man, and yet I really can name nothing out of the way. No, sir; I can make no hand of it; I can't describe him. And it's not want of memory; for I declare I can see him this moment."

Mr. Utterson again walked some way in silence and obviously under a weight of consideration. "You are sure he used a key?" he inquired at last.

"My dear sir . . ." began Enfield, surprised out of himself.

"Yes, I know," said Utterson; "I know it must seem strange. The fact is, if I do not ask you the name of the other party, it is because I know it already. You see, Richard, your tale has gone home. If you have been inexact in any point, you had better correct it."

"I think you might have warned me," returned the other with a touch of sullenness. "But I have been pedantically exact, as you call it. The fellow had a key; and what's more, he has it still. I saw him use it, not a week ago."

Mr. Utterson sighed deeply but said never a word; and the young man presently resumed. "Here is another lesson to say nothing," said he. "I am ashamed of my long tongue. Let us make a bargain never to refer to this again."

"With all my heart," said the lawyer. "I shake hands on that, Richard."

Search for Mr. Hyde

THAT evening Mr. Utterson came home to his bachelor house in sombre spirits and sat down to dinner without relish. It was his custom of a Sunday, when this meal was over, to sit close by the fire, a volume of some dry divinity on his reading desk, until the clock of the neighbouring church rang out the hour of twelve, when he would go soberly and gratefully to bed. On this night, however, as soon as the cloth was taken away, he took up a candle and went into his business room. There he opened his safe, took from the most private part of it a document endorsed on the envelope as Dr. Jekyll's Will, and sat down with a clouded brow to study its contents. The will was holograph, for Mr. Utterson, though he took charge of it now that it was made, had refused to lend the least assistance in the making of it; it provided not only that, in case of the decease of Henry Jekyll, M.D., D.C.L., L.L.D., F.R.S., etc., all his possessions were to pass into the hands of his "friend and benefactor Edward Hyde," but that in case of Dr. Jekyll's "disappearance or unexplained absence for any period exceeding three calendar months," the said Edward Hyde should step into the said Henry Jekyll's shoes without further delay and free from any burthen or obligation, beyond the payment of a few small sums to the members of the doctor's household. This document had long been the lawyer's eyesore. It offended him both as a lawyer and as a lover of the sane and customary sides of life, to whom the fanciful was the immodest. And hitherto it was his ignorance of Mr. Hyde that had swelled his indignation; now, by a sudden turn, it was his knowledge. It was already bad enough when the name was but a name of which he could learn no more. It was worse when it began to be clothed upon with destestable attributes; and out of the shifting, insubstantial mists that had so long baffled his eye, there leaped up the sudden, definite presentment of a fiend.

"I thought it was madness," he said, as he replaced the obnoxious paper in the safe, "and now I begin to fear it is disgrace."

With that he blew out his candle, put on a greatcoat, and set forth in the direction of Cavendish Square, that citadel of medicine, where his friend, the great Dr. Lanyon, had his house and received his crowding patients. "If anyone knows, it will be Lanyon," he had thought.

The solemn butler knew and welcomed him; he was subjected to no stage of delay, but ushered direct from the door to the dining-room where Dr. Lanyon sat alone over his wine. This was a hearty, healthy, dapper, red-faced gentleman, with a shock of hair prematurely white, and a boisterous and decided manner. At sight of Mr. Utterson, he sprang

up from his chair and welcomed him with both
hands. The geniality, as was the way of the man,
was somewhat theatrical to the eye; but it reposed
on genuine feeling. For these two were old friends,
old mates both at school and college, both thorough
respectors of themselves and of each other, and
what does not always follow, men who thoroughly
enjoyed each other's company.

After a little rambling talk, the lawyer led up
to the subject which so disagreeably preoccupied
his mind.

"I suppose, Lanyon," said he, "you and I must be
the two oldest friends that Henry Jekyll has?"

"I wish the friends were younger," chuckled Dr.
Lanyon. "But I suppose we are. And what of that?
I see little of him now."

"Indeed?" said Utterson. "I thought you had a
bond of common interest."

"We had," was the reply. "But it is more than
ten years since Henry Jekyll became too fanciful
for me. He began to go wrong, wrong in mind;
and though of course I continue to take an interest
in him for old sake's sake, as they say, I see and
I have seen devilish little of the man. Such unscien-
tific balderdash," added the doctor, flushing suddenly purple, "would have estranged Damon and
Pythias."

This little spirit of temper was somewhat of a relief to Mr. Utterson. "They have only differed on
some point of science," he thought; and being a
man of no scientific passions (except in the matter

of conveyancing), he even added: "It is nothing worse than that!" He gave his friend a few seconds to recover his composure, and then approached the question he had come to put. "Did you ever come across a protégé of his—one Hyde?" he asked.

"Hyde?" repeated Lanyon. "No. Never heard of him. Since my time."

That was the amount of information that the lawyer carried back with him to the great, dark bed on which he tossed to and fro, until the small hours of the morning began to grow large. It was a night of little ease to his toiling mind, toiling in mere darkness and beseiged by questions.

Six o'clock struck on the bells of the church that was so conveniently near to Mr. Utterson's dwelling, and still he was digging at the problem. Hitherto it had touched him on the intellectual side alone; but now his imagination also was engaged, or rather enslaved; and as he lay and tossed in the gross darkness of the night and the curtained room, Mr. Enfield's tale went by before his mind in a scroll of lighted pictures. He would be aware of the great field of lamps of a nocturnal city; then of the figure of a man walking swiftly; then of a child running from the doctor's; and then these met, and that human Juggernaut trod the child down and passed on regardless of her screams. Or else he would see a room in a rich house, where his friend lay asleep, dreaming and smiling at his dreams; and then the door of that room would be opened, the curtains of the bed plucked apart, the

sleeper recalled, and lo! there would stand by his
side a figure to whom power was given, and even
at that dead hour, he must rise and do its bidding.
The figure in these two phases haunted the lawyer
all night; and if at any time he dozed over, it
was but to see it glide more stealthily through
sleeping houses, or move the more swiftly and still
the more swiftly, even to dizziness, through wider
labyrinths of lamplighted city, and at every street
corner crush a child and leave her screaming. And
still the figure had no face by which he might know
it; even in his dreams, it had no face, or one that
baffled him and melted before his eyes; and thus it
was that there sprang up and grew apace in the
lawyer's mind a singularly strong, almost an inordinate, curiosity to behold the features of the real
Mr. Hyde. If he could but once set eyes on him,
he thought the mystery would lighten and perhaps
roll altogether away, as was the habit of mysterious
things when well examined. He might see a reason
for his friend's strange preference or bondage (call
it which you please) and even for the startling
clause of the will. At least it would be a face worth
seeing: the face of a man who was without bowels
of mercy: a face which had but to show itself to
raise up, in the mind of the unimpressionable Enfield, a spirit of enduring hatred.

From that time forward, Mr. Utterson began to
haunt the door in the by-street of shops. In the
morning before office hours, at noon when business
was plenty, and time scarce, at night under the

face of the fogged city moon, by all lights and at all hours of solitude or concourse, the lawyer was to be found on his chosen post.

"If he be Mr. Hyde," he had thought, "I shall be Mr. Seek."

And at last his patience was rewarded. It was a fine dry night; frost in the air; the streets as clean as a ballroom floor; the lamps, unshaken by any wind, drawing a regular pattern of light and shadow. By ten o'clock, when the shops were closed, the by-street was very solitary and, in spite of the low growl of London from all round, very silent. Small sounds carried far; domestic sounds out of the houses were clearly audible on either side of the roadway; and the rumour of the approach of any passenger preceded him by a long time. Mr. Utterson had been some minutes at his post, when he was aware of an odd, light footstep drawing near. In the course of his nightly patrols, he had long grown accustomed to the quaint effect with which the footfalls of a single person, while he is still a great way off, suddenly spring out distinct from the vast hum and clatter of the city. Yet his attention had never before been so sharply and decisively arrested; and it was with a strong, superstitious prevision of success that he withdrew into the entry of the court.

The steps drew swiftly nearer, and swelled out suddenly louder as they turned the end of the street. The lawyer, looking forth from the entry, could soon see what manner of man he had to deal

with. He was small and very plainly dressed, and
the look of him, even at that distance, went somehow strongly against the watcher's inclination. But
he made straight for the door, crossing the roadway to save time; and as he came, he drew a key
from his pocket like one approaching home.

Mr. Utterson stepped out and touched him on
the shoulder as he passed. "Mr. Hyde, I think?"

Mr. Hyde shrank back with a hissing intake of
the breath. But his fear was only momentary; and
though he did not look the lawyer in the face, he
answered coolly enough: "That is my name. What
do you want?"

"I see you are going in," returned the lawyer. "I
am an old friend of Dr. Jekyll's—Mr. Utterson of
Gaunt Street—you must have heard of my name;
and meeting you so conveniently, I thought you
might admit me."

"You will not find Dr. Jekyll; he is from home,"
replied Mr. Hyde, blowing in the key. And then
suddenly, but still without looking up, "How did
you know me?" he asked.

"On your side," said Mr. Utterson, "will you do
me a favour?"

"With pleasure," replied the other. "What shall
it be?"

"Will you let me see your face?" asked the lawyer.

Mr. Hyde appeared to hesitate, and then, as if
upon some sudden reflection, fronted about with
an air of defiance; and the pair stared at each
other pretty fixedly for a few seconds. "Now I shall

know you again," said Mr. Utterson. "It may be useful."

"Yes," returned Mr. Hyde, "it is as well we have met; and *à propos,* you should have my address." And he gave a number of a street in Soho.

"Good God!" thought Mr. Utterson, "can he, too, have been thinking of the will?" But he kept his feelings to himself and only grunted in acknowledgment of the address.

"And now," said the other, "how did you know me?"

"By description," was the reply.

"Whose description?"

"We have common friends," said Mr. Utterson.

"Common friends?" echoed Mr. Hyde, a little hoarsely. "Who are they?"

"Jekyll, for instance," said the lawyer.

"He never told you," cried Mr. Hyde, with a flush of anger. "I did not think you would have lied."

"Come," said Mr. Utterson, "that is not fitting language."

The other snarled aloud into a savage laugh; and the next moment, with extraordinary quickness, he had unlocked the door and disappeared into the house.

The lawyer stood awhile when Mr. Hyde had left him, the picture of disquietude. Then he began slowly to mount the street, pausing every step or two and putting his hand to his brow like a man in mental perplexity. The problem he was thus de-

bating as he walked, was one of a class that is
rarely solved. Mr. Hyde was pale and dwarfish, he
gave an impression of deformity without any nameable malformation, he had a displeasing smile, he
had borne himself to the lawyer with a sort of
murderous mixture of timidity and boldness, and
he spoke with a husky, whispering and somewhat
broken voice; all these were points against him, but
not all of these together could explain the hitherto
unknown disgust, loathing and fear with which Mr.
Utterson regarded him. "There must be something
else," said the perplexed gentleman. "There *is*
something more, if I could find a name for it. God
bless me, the man seems hardly human! Something
troglodytic, shall we say? or can it be the old story
of Dr. Fell? or is it the mere radiance of a foul soul
that thus transpires through, and transfigures, its
clay continent? The last, I think; for, O my poor
old Harry Jekyll, if ever I read Satan's signature
upon a face, it is on that of your new friend."

Round the corner from the by-street, there was a
square of ancient, handsome houses, now for the
most part decayed from their high estate and let in
flats and chambers to all sorts and conditions of
men; map-engravers, architects, shady lawyers and
the agents of obscure enterprises. One house, however, second from the corner, was still occupied
entire; and at the door of this, which wore a great
air of wealth and comfort, though it was now
plunged in darkness except for the fanlight, Mr.

Utterson stopped and knocked. A well-dressed, elderly servant opened the door.

"Is Dr. Jekyll at home, Poole?" asked the lawyer.

"I will see, Mr. Utterson," said Poole, admitting the visitor, as he spoke, into a large, low-roofed, comfortable hall, paved with flags, warmed (after the fashion of a country house) by a bright, open fire, and furnished with costly cabinets of oak. "Will you wait here by the fire, sir? or shall I give you a light in the dining-room?"

"Here, thank you," said the lawyer, and he drew near and leaned on the tall fender. This hall, in which he was now left alone, was a pet fancy of his friend the doctor's; and Utterson himself was wont to speak of it as the pleasantest room in London. But tonight there was a shudder in his blood; the face of Hyde sat heavy on his memory; he felt (what was rare with him) a nausea and distaste of life; and in the gloom of his spirits, he seemed to read a menace in the flickering of the firelight on the polished cabinets and the uneasy starting of the shadow on the roof. He was ashamed of his relief, when Poole presently returned to announce that Dr. Jekyll was gone out.

"I saw Mr. Hyde go in by the old dissecting-room door, Poole," he said. "Is that right, when Dr. Jekyll is from home?"

"Quite right, Mr. Utterson, sir," replied the servant. "Mr. Hyde has a key."

"Your master seems to repose a great deal of

trust in that young man, Poole," resumed the other musingly.

"Yes, sir, he does indeed," said Poole. "We have all orders to obey him."

"I do not think I ever met Mr. Hyde?" asked Utterson.

"O, dear no, sir. He never *dines* here," replied the butler. "Indeed we see very little of him on this side of the house; he mostly comes and goes by the laboratory."

"Well, good-night, Poole."

"Good-night, Mr. Utterson."

And the lawyer set out homeward with a very heavy heart. "Poor Harry Jekyl," he thought, "my mind misgives me he is in deep waters! He was wild when he was young; a long while ago to be sure; but in the law of God, there is no statute of limitations. Ay, it must be that; the ghost of some old sin, the cancer of some concealed disgrace: punishment coming, *pede claudo*, years after memory has forgotten and self-love condoned the fault." And the lawyer, scared by the thought, brooded awhile on his own past, groping in all the corners of memory, lest by chance some Jack-in-the-Box of an old iniquity should leap to light there. His past was fairly blameless; few men could read the rolls of their life with less apprehension; yet he was humbled to the dust by the many ill things he had done, and raised up again into a sober and fearful gratitude by the many he had come so near to doing, yet avoided. And then by a return on his former subject, he conceived a spark of hope. "This Master Hyde, if he were studied," thought he, "must have secrets of his own; black secrets, by the look of him; secrets compared to which poor Jekyll's worst would be like sunshine. Things cannot continue as they are. It turns me cold to think of this creature stealing like a thief to Harry's bedside; poor Harry, what a wakening! And the danger of it; for if this Hyde suspects the existence of the will, he may grow impatient to inherit. Ay, I must put my shoulders to the wheel— if Jekyll will but let me," he added, "if Jekyll will only let me." For once more he saw before his mind's eye, as clear as transparency, the strange clauses of the will.

Dr. Jekyll Was Quite at Ease

A FORTNIGHT later, by excellent good fortune, the doctor gave one of his pleasant dinners to some five or six old cronies, all intelligent, reputable men and all judges of good wine; and Mr. Utterson so contrived that he remained behind after the others had departed. This was no new arrangement, but a thing that had befallen many scores of times. Where Utterson was liked, he was liked well. Hosts loved to detain the dry lawyer, when the light-hearted and loose-tongued had already their foot on the threshold; they liked to sit awhile in his unobtrusive company, practising for solitude, sobering their minds in the man's rich silence after the expense and strain of gaiety. To this rule, Dr. Jekyll was no exception; and as he now sat on the opposite side of the fire—a large, well-made, smooth-faced man of fifty, with something of a slyish cast perhaps, but every mark of capacity and kindness—you could see by his looks that he cherished for Mr. Utterson a sincere and warm affection.

"I have been wanting to speak to you, Jekyll," began the latter. "You know that will of yours?"

A close observer might have gathered that the topic was distasteful; but the doctor carried it off gaily. "My poor Utterson," said he, "you are unfortunate in such a client. I never saw a man so distressed as you were by my will; unless it were that hide-bound pedant, Lanyon, at what he called my scientific heresies. O, I know he's a good fellow—you needn't frown—an excellent fellow, and I always mean to see more of him; but a hidebound pedant for all that; an ignorant, blatant pedant. I was never more disappointed in any man than Lanyon."

"You know I never approved of it," pursued Utterson, ruthlessly disregarding the fresh topic.

"My will? Yes, certainly, I know that," said the doctor, a trifle sharply. "You have told me so."

"Well, I tell you so again," continued the lawyer. "I have been learning something of young Hyde."

The large handsome face of Dr. Jekyll grew pale to the very lips, and there came a blackness about his eyes. "I do not care to hear more," said he. "This is a matter I thought we had agreed to drop."

"What I heard was abominable," said Utterson.

"It can make no change. You do not understand my position," returned the doctor, with a certain incoherency of manner. "I am painfully situated, Utterson; my position is a very strange—a very strange one. It is one of those affairs that cannot be mended by talking."

"Jekyll," said Utterson, "you know me: I am a man to be trusted. Make a clean breast of this in confidence; and I make no doubt I can get you out of it."

"My good Utterson," said the doctor, "this is very good of you, this is downright good of you, and I cannot find words to thank you in. I believe you fully; I would trust you before any man alive, ay, before myself, if I could make the choice; but indeed it isn't what you fancy; it is not as bad as that; and just to put your good heart at rest, I will tell you one thing: the moment I choose, I can be rid of Mr. Hyde. I give you my hand upon that; and I thank you again and again; and I will just add one little word, Utterson, that I'm sure you'll take in good part: this is a private matter, and I beg of you to let it sleep."

Utterson reflected a little, looking in the fire.

"I have no doubt you are perfectly right," he said at last, getting to his feet.

"Well, but since we have touched upon this business, and for the last time I hope," continued the doctor, "there is one point I should like you to understand. I have really a very great interest in poor Hyde. I know you have seen him; he told me so; and I fear he was rude. But I do sincerely take a great, a very great interest in that young man; and if I am taken away, Utterson, I wish you to promise me that you will bear with him and get his rights for him. I think you would, if you knew all; and it would be a weight off my mind if you would promise."

"I can't pretend that I shall ever like him," said the lawyer.

"I don't ask that," pleaded Jekyll, laying his

hand upon the other's arm; "I only ask for justice;
I only ask you to help him for my sake, when I am
no longer here."

Utterson heaved an irrepressible sigh. "Well,"
said he, "I promise."

The Carew Murder Case

NEARLY a year later, in the month of October, 18—, London was startled by a crime of singular ferocity and rendered all the more notable by the high position of the victim. The details were few and startling. A maid servant living alone in a house not far from the river, had gone upstairs to bed about eleven. Although a fog rolled over the city in the small hours, the early part of the night was cloudless, and the lane, which the maid's window overlooked, was brilliantly lit by the full moon. It seems she was romantically given, for she sat down upon her box, which stood immediately under the window, and fell into a dream of musing. Never (she used to say, with streaming tears, when she narrated that experience), never had she felt more at peace with all men or thought more kindly of the world. And as she so sat she became aware of an aged beautiful gentleman with white hair, drawing near along the lane; and advancing to meet him, another and very small gentleman, to whom at first she paid less attention. When they had come within speech (which was just under the maid's eyes) the older man bowed and accosted the other with a very pretty manner of politeness. It did not seem as if the subject of his address were of great importance; indeed, from his pointing, it sometimes appeared as if he were only inquiring his way; but the moon shone on his face as he spoke, and the girl was pleased to watch it, it seemed to breathe such an innocent and old-world kindness of disposition, yet with something high too, as of a well-founded self-content. Presently her eye wandered to the other, and she was surprised to recognise in him a certain Mr. Hyde, who had once visited her master and for whom she had conceived a dislike. He had in his hand a heavy cane, with which he was trifling; but he answered never a word, and seemed to listen with an ill-contained impatience. And then all of a sudden he broke out in a great flame of anger, stamping with his foot, brandishing the cane, and carrying on (as the maid described it) like a madman. The old gentleman took a step back, with the air of one very much surprised and a trifle hurt; and at that Mr. Hyde broke out of all bounds and clubbed him to the earth. And next moment, with ape-like fury, he was trampling his victim under foot and hailing down a storm of blows, under which the bones were audibly shattered and the body jumped upon the roadway. At the horror of these sights and sounds, the maid fainted.

It was two o'clock when she came to herself and called for the police. The murderer was gone long ago; but there lay his victim in the middle of the lane, incredibly mangled. The stick with which the deed had been done, although it was of some rare and very tough and heavy wood, had broken in the

middle under the stress of this insensate cruelty;
and one splintered half had rolled in the neighbouring gutter—the other, without doubt, had been
carried away by the murderer. A purse and gold
watch were found upon the victim: but no cards
or papers, except a sealed and stamped envelope,
which he had been probably carrying to the post,
and which bore the name and address of Mr. Utterson.

This was brought to the lawyer the next morning,
before he was out of bed; and he had no sooner
seen it, and been told the circumstances, than he
shot out a solemn lip. "I shall say nothing till I have
seen the body," said he; "this may be very serious.
Have the kindness to wait while I dress." And
with the same grave countenance he hurried
through his breakfast and drove to the police
station, whither the body had been carried. As soon
as he came into the cell, he nodded.

"Yes," said he, "I recognise him. I am sorry to
say that this is Sir Danvers Carew."

"Good God, sir," exclaimed the officer, "is it
possible?" And the next moment his eye lighted
up with professional ambition. "This will make a
deal of noise," he said. "And perhaps you can help
us to the man." And he briefly narrated what the
maid had seen, and showed the broken stick.

Mr. Utterson had already quailed at the name
of Hyde; but when the stick was laid before him,
he could doubt no longer; broken and battered as

it was, he recognized it for one that he had himself presented many years before to Henry Jekyll.

"Is this Mr. Hyde a person of small stature?" he inquired.

"Particularly small and particularly wicked-looking, is what the maid calls him," said the officer.

Mr. Utterson reflected; and then, raising his head, "If you will come with me in my cab," he said, "I think I can take you to his house."

It was by this time about nine in the morning, and the first fog of the season. A great chocolate-coloured pall lowered over heaven, but the wind was continually charging and routing these embattled vapours; so that as the cab crawled from street to street, Mr. Utterson beheld a marvelous number of degrees and hues of twilight; for here it would be dark like the back-end of evening; and there would be a glow of a rich, lurid brown, like the light of some strange conflagration; and here, for a moment, the fog would be quite broken up, and a haggard shaft of daylight would glance in between the swirling wreaths. The dismal quarter of Soho seen under these changing glimpses, with its muddy ways, and slatternly passengers, and its lamps, which had never been extinguished or had been kindled afresh to combat this mournful reinvasion of darkness, seemed, in the lawyer's eyes, like a district of some city in a nightmare. The thoughts of his mind, besides, were of the gloomiest dye; and when he glanced at the companion of his drive, he was conscious of some touch of that terror of the law and the law's officers, which may at times assail the most honest.

As the cab drew up before the address indicated, the fog lifted a little and showed him a dingy street, a gin palace, a low French eating house, a shop for the retail of penny numbers and twopenny salads, many ragged children huddled in the doorways, and many women of many different nationalities passing out, key in hand, to have a morning glass; and the next moment the fog settled down again upon that part, as brown as umber, and cut him off from his blackguardly surroundings. This was the home of Henry Jekyll's favourite; of a man who was heir to a quarter of a million sterling.

An ivory-faced and silvery-haired old woman opened the door. She had an evil face, smoothed by hypocrisy: but her manners were excellent. Yes, she said, this was Mr. Hyde's, but he was not at home; he had been in that night very late, but he had gone away again in less than an hour; there was nothing strange in that; his habits were very irregular, and he was often absent; for instance, it was nearly two months since she had seen him till yesterday.

"Very well, then, we wish to see his rooms," said the lawyer; and when the woman began to declare it was impossible, "I had better tell you who this person is," he added. "This is Inspector Newcomen of Scotland Yard."

A flash of odious joy appeared upon the woman's

face. "Ah!" said she, "he is in trouble! What has he done?"

Mr. Utterson and the inspector exchanged glances. "He don't seem a very popular character," observed the latter. "And now, my good woman, just let me and this gentleman have a look about us."

In the whole extent of the house, which but for the old woman remained otherwise empty, Mr. Hyde had only used a couple of rooms; but these were furnished with luxury and good taste. A closet was filled with wine; the plate was of silver, the napery elegant; a good picture hung upon the walls, a gift (as Utterson supposed) from Henry Jekyll, who was much of a connoisseur; and the carpets were of many plies and agreeable in colour. At this moment, however, the rooms bore every mark of having been recently and hurriedly ransacked; clothes lay about the floor, with their pockets inside out; lock-fast drawers stood open; and on the hearth there lay a pile of grey ashes, as though many papers had been burned. From these embers the inspector disinterred the butt end of a green cheque book, which had resisted the action of the fire; the other half of the stick was found behind the door; and as this clinched his suspicions, the officer declared himself delighted. A visit to the bank, where several thousand pounds were found to be lying to the murderer's credit, completed his gratification.

"You may depend upon it, sir," he told Mr. Utter-

son: "I have him in my hand. He must have lost his
head, or he never would have left the stick or,
above all, burned the cheque book. Why, money's
life to the man. We have nothing to do but wait for
him at the bank, and get out the handbills."

This last, however, was not so easy of accomplish-
ment; for Mr. Hyde had numbered few familiars
—even the master of the servant maid had only seen
him twice; his family could nowhere be traced; he
had never been photographed; and the few who
could describe him differed widely, as common ob-
servers will. Only on one point were they agreed;
and that was the haunting sense of unexpressed
deformity with which the fugitive impressed his
beholders.

Incident of the Letter

It was late in the afternoon, when Mr. Utterson found his way to Dr. Jekyll's door, where he was at once admitted by Poole, and carried down by the kitchen offices and across a yard which had once been a garden, to the building which was indifferently known as the laboratory or dissecting rooms. The doctor had bought the house from the heirs of a celebrated surgeon; and his own tastes being rather chemical than anatomical, had changed the destination of the block at the bottom of the garden. It was the first time that the lawyer had been received in that part of his friend's quarters; and he eyed the dingy, windowless structure with curiosity, and gazed round with a distasteful sense of strangeness as he crossed the theatre, once crowded with eager students and now lying gaunt and silent, the tables laden with chemical apparatus, the floor strewn with crates and littered with packing straw, and the light falling dimly through the foggy cupola. At the further end, a flight of stairs mounted to a door covered with red baize; and through this, Mr. Utterson was at last received into the doctor's cabinet. It was a large room fitted round with glass presses, furnished, among other things, with a cheval-glass and a business table, and looking out upon the court by three dusty windows barred with iron. The fire burned in the grate; a lamp was set lighted on the chimney shelf, for even in the houses the fog began to lie thickly; and there, close up to the warmth, sat Dr. Jekyll, looking deathly sick. He did not rise to meet his visitor, but held out a cold hand and bade him welcome in a changed voice.

"And now," said Mr. Utterson, as soon as Poole had left them, "you have heard the news?"

The doctor shuddered. "They were crying it in the square," he said. "I heard them in my dining-room."

"One word," said the lawyer. "Carew was my client, but so are you, and I want to know what I am doing. You have not been mad enough to hide this fellow?"

"Utterson, I swear to God," cried the doctor, "I swear to God I will never set eyes on him again. I bind my honour to you that I am done with him in this world. It is all at an end. And indeed he does not want my help; you do not know him as I do; he is safe, he is quite safe; mark my words, he will never more be heard of."

The lawyer listened gloomily; he did not like his friend's feverish manner. "You seem pretty sure of him," said he; "and for your sake, I hope you may be right. If it came to a trial, your name might appear."

"I am quite sure of him," replied Jekyll; "I have grounds for certainty that I cannot share with anyone. But there is one thing on which you may advise me. I have—I have received a letter; and I am at a loss whether I should show it to the police. I should like to leave it in your hands, Utterson; you would judge wisely, I am sure; I have so great a trust in you."

"You fear, I suppose, that it might lead to his detection?" asked the lawyer.

"No," said the other. "I cannot say that I care what becomes of Hyde; I am quite done with him. I was thinking of my own character, which this hateful business has rather exposed."

Utterson ruminated awhile; he was surprised at his friend's selfishness, and yet relieved by it. "Well," said he, at last, "let me see the letter."

The letter was written in an odd, upright hand and signed "Edward Hyde": and it signified, briefly enough, that the writer's benefactor, Dr. Jekyll, whom he had long so unworthily repaid for a thousand generosities, need labour under no alarm for his safety, as he had means of escape on which he placed a sure dependence. The lawyer liked this letter well enough; it put a better colour on the intimacy than he had looked for; and he blamed himself for some of his past suspicions.

"Have you the envelope?" he asked.

"I burned it," replied Jekyll, "before I thought what I was about. But it bore no postmark. The note was handed in."

"Shall I keep this and sleep upon it?" asked Utterson.

"I wish you to judge for me entirely," was the reply. "I have lost confidence in myself."

"Well, I shall consider," returned the lawyer. "And now one word more: it was Hyde who dictated the terms in your will about that disappearance?"

The doctor seemed seized with a qualm of faintness; he shut his mouth tight and nodded.

"I knew it," said Utterson. "He meant to murder you. You had a fine escape."

"I have had what is far more to the purpose," returned the doctor solemnly: "I have had a lesson—O God, Utterson, what a lesson I have had!" And he covered his face for a moment with his hands.

On his way out, the lawyer stopped and had a word or two with Poole. "By the bye," said he, "there was a letter handed in to-day: what was the messenger like?" But Poole was positive nothing had come except by post; "and only circulars by that," he added.

This news sent off the visitor with his fears renewed. Plainly the letter had come by the laboratory door; possibly, indeed, it had been written in the cabinet; and if that were so, it must be differently judged, and handled with the more caution. The newsboys, as he went, were crying themselves hoarse along the footways: "Special edition. Shocking murder of an M.P." That was the funeral oration of one friend and client; and he could not help a certain apprehension lest the good name of another should be sucked down in the eddy of the

scandal. It was, at least, a ticklish decision that he
had to make; and self-reliant as he was by habit, he
began to cherish a longing for advice. It was not to
be had directly; but perhaps, he thought, it might
be fished for.

Presently after, he sat on one side of his own
hearth, with Mr. Guest, his head clerk, upon the
other, and midway between, at a nicely calculated
distance from the fire, a bottle of a particular old
wine that had long dwelt unsunned in the founda-
tions of his house. The fog still slept on the wing
above the drowned city, where the lamps glim-
mered like carbuncles; and through the muffle and
smother of these fallen clouds, the procession of
the town's life was still rolling in through the great
arteries with a sound as of a mighty wind. But the
room was gay with firelight. In the bottle the acids
were long ago resolved; the imperial dye had
softened with time, as the colour grows richer in
stained windows; and the glow of hot autumn
afternoons on hillside vineyards, was ready to be
set free and to disperse the fogs of London. In-
sensibly the lawyer melted. There was no man
from whom he kept fewer secrets than Mr. Guest;
and he was not always sure that he kept as many as
he meant. Guest had often been on business to the
doctor's; he knew Poole; he could scarce have
failed to hear of Mr. Hyde's familiarity about the
house; he might draw conclusions: was it not as
well, then, that he should see a letter which put that
mystery to rights? and above all since Guest, being

a great student and critic of handwriting, would
consider the step natural and obliging? The clerk,
besides, was a man of counsel; he could scarce
read so strange a document without dropping a remark; and by that remark Mr. Utterson might
shape his future course.

"This is a sad business about Sir Danvers," he
said.

"Yes, sir, indeed. It has elicited a great deal of
public feeling," returned Guest. "The man, of
course, was mad."

"I should like to hear your views on that," replied
Utterson. "I have a document here in his handwriting; it is between ourselves, for I scarce know
what to do about it; it is an ugly business at the
best. But there it is; quite in your way: a murderer's autograph."

Guest's eyes brightened, and he sat down at once
and studied it with passion. "No sir," he said: "not
mad; but it is an odd hand."

"And by all accounts a very odd writer," added
the lawyer.

Just then the servant entered with a note.

"Is that from Dr. Jekyll, sir?" inquired the clerk.
"I thought I knew the writing. Anything private,
Mr. Utterson?"

"Only an invitation to dinner. Why? Do you want
to see it?"

"One moment. I thank you, sir;" and the clerk
laid the two sheets of paper alongside and sedu-
lously compared their contents. "Thank you, sir," he

said at last, returning both; "it's a very interesting autograph."

There was a pause, during which Mr. Utterson struggled with himself. "Why did you compare them, Guest?" he inquired suddenly.

"Well, sir," returned the clerk, "there's a rather singular resemblance; the two hands are in many points identical: only differently sloped."

"Rather quaint," said Utterson.

"It is, as you say, rather quaint," returned Guest.

"I wouldn't speak of this note, you know," said the master.

"No, sir," said the clerk. "I understand."

But no sooner was Mr. Utterson alone that night, than he locked the note into his safe, where it reposed from that time forward. "What!" he thought. "Henry Jekyll forge for a murderer!" And his blood ran cold in his veins.

Remarkable Incident of Dr. Lanyon

TIME ran on; thousands of pounds were offered in reward, for the death of Sir Danvers was resented as a public injury; but Mr. Hyde had disappeared out of the ken of the police as though he had never existed. Much of his past was unearthed, indeed, and all disreputable: tales came out of the man's cruelty, at once so callous and violent; of his vile life, of his strange associates, of the hatred that seemed to have surrounded his career; but of his present whereabouts, not a whisper. From the time he had left the house in Soho on the morning of the murder, he was simply blotted out; and gradually, as time drew on, Mr. Utterson began to recover from the hotness of his alarm, and to grow more at quiet with himself. The death of Sir Danvers was, to his way of thinking, more than paid for by the disappearance of Mr. Hyde. Now that that evil influence had been withdrawn, a new life began for Dr. Jekyll. He came out of his seclusion, renewed relations with his friends, became once more their familiar guest and entertainer; and whilst he had always been known for charities, he was now no less distinguished for religion. He was busy, he was much in the open air, he did good; his face seemed to open and brighten, as if with an inward consciousness of service; and for more than two months, the doctor was at peace.

On the 8th of January Utterson had dined at the doctor's with a small party; Lanyon had been there; and the face of the host had looked from one to the other as in the old days when the trio were inseparable friends. On the 12th, and again on the 14th, the door was shut against the lawyer. "The doctor was confined to the house," Poole said, "and saw no one." On the 15th, he tried again, and was again refused; and having now been used for the last two months to see his friend almost daily, he found this return of solitude to weigh upon his spirits. The fifth night he had in Guest to dine with him; and the sixth he betook himself to Dr. Lanyon's.

There at least he was not denied admittance; but when he came in, he was shocked at the change which had taken place in the doctor's appearance. He had his death-warrant written legibly upon his face. The rosy man had grown pale; his flesh had fallen away; he was visibly balder and older; and yet it was not so much these tokens of a swift physical decay that arrested the lawyer's notice, as a look in the eye and quality of manner that seemed to testify to some deep-seated terror of the mind. It was unlikely that the doctor should fear death; and yet that was what Utterson was tempted to suspect. "Yes," he thought; "he is a doctor, he must know his own state and that his days are counted;

and the knowledge is more than he can bear."
And yet when Utterson remarked on his ill-looks,
it was with an air of great firmness that Lanyon
declared himself a doomed man.

"I have had a shock," he said, "and I shall never
recover. It is a question of weeks. Well, life has
been pleasant; I liked it; yes, sir, I used to like it. I
sometimes think if we knew all, we should be
more glad to get away."

"Jekyll is ill, too," observed Utterson. "Have you
seen him?"

But Lanyon's face changed, and he held up a
trembling hand. "I wish to see or hear no more of
Dr. Jekyll," he said in a loud, unsteady voice. "I
am quite done with that person; and I beg that you
will spare me any allusion to one whom I regard as
dead."

"Tut-tut," said Mr. Utterson; and then after a
considerable pause, "Can't I do anything?" he inquired. "We are three very old friends, Lanyon; we
shall not live to make others."

"Nothing can be done," returned Lanyon; "ask
himself."

"He will not see me," said the lawyer.

"I am not surprised at that," was the reply. "Some
day, Utterson, after I am dead, you may perhaps
come to learn the right and wrong of this. I cannot
tell you. And in the meantime, if you can sit and
talk with me of other things, for God's sake, stay
and do so; but if you cannot keep clear of this

accursed topic, then in God's name, go, for I cannot bear it."

As soon as he got home, Utterson sat down and wrote to Jekyll, complaining of his exclusion from the house, and asking the cause of this unhappy break with Lanyon; and the next day brought him a long answer, often very pathetically worded, and sometimes darkly mysterious in drift. The quarrel with Lanyon was incurable. "I do not blame our old friend," Jekyll wrote, "but I share his view that we must never meet. I mean from henceforth to lead a life of extreme seclusion; you must not be surprised, nor must you doubt my friendship, if my door is often shut even to you. You must suffer me to go my own dark way. I have brought on myself a punishment and a danger that I cannot name. If I am the chief of sinners, I am the chief of sufferers also. I could not think that this earth contained a place for sufferings and terrors so unmanning; and you can do but one thing, Utterson, to lighten this destiny, and that is to respect my silence." Utterson was amazed; the dark influence of Hyde had been withdrawn, the doctor had returned to his old tasks and amities; a week ago, the prospect had smiled with every promise of a cheerful and an honoured age; and now in a moment, friendship, and peace of mind, and the whole tenor of his life were wrecked. So great and unprepared a change pointed to madness; but in view of Lanyon's manner and words, there must lie for it some deeper ground.

A week afterwards Dr. Lanyon took to his bed, and in something less than a fortnight he was dead. The night after the funeral, at which he had been sadly affected, Utterson locked the door of his business room, and sitting there by the light of a melancholy candle, drew out and set before him an envelope addressed by the hand and sealed with the seal of his dead friend. "PRIVATE: for the hands of G. J. Utterson ALONE, and in case of his predecease *to be destroyed unread*," so it was emphatically superscribed; and the lawyer dreaded to behold the contents. "I have buried one friend to-day," he thought: "what if this should cost me another?" And then he condemned the fear as a disloyalty, and broke the seal. Within there was another enclosure, likewise sealed, and marked upon the cover as "not to be opened till the death or disappearance of Dr. Henry Jekyll." Utterson could not trust his eyes. Yes, it was disappearance; here again, as in the mad will which he had long ago restored to its author, here again were the idea of a disappearance and the name of Henry Jekyll bracketted. But in the will, that idea had sprung from the sinister suggestion of the man Hyde; it was set there with a purpose all too plain and horrible. Written by the hand of Lanyon, what should it mean? A great curiosity came on the trustee, to disregard the prohibition and dive at once to the bottom of these mysteries; but professional honour and faith to his dead friend were stringent obligations; and the packet slept in the inmost corner of his private safe.

It is one thing to mortify curiosity, another to conquer it; and it may be doubted if, from that day forth, Utterson desired the society of his surviving friend with the same eagerness. He thought of him kindly; but his thoughts were disquieted and fearful. He went to call indeed; but he was perhaps relieved to be denied admittance; perhaps, in his heart, he preferred to speak with Poole upon the doorstep and surrounded by the air and sounds of the open city, rather than to be admitted into that house of voluntary bondage, and to sit and speak with its inscrutable recluse. Poole had, indeed, no very pleasant news to communicate. The doctor, it appeared, now more than ever confined himself to the cabinet over the laboratory, where he would sometimes even sleep; he was out of spirits, he had grown very silent, he did not read; it seemed as if he had something on his mind. Utterson became so used to the unvarying character of these reports, that he fell off little by little in the frequency of his visits.

Incident at the Window

It chanced on Sunday, when Mr. Utterson was on his usual walk with Mr. Enfield, that their way lay once again through the by-street; and that when they came in front of the door, both stopped to gaze on it.

"Well," said Enfield, "that story's at an end at least. We shall never see more of Mr. Hyde."

"I hope not," said Utterson. "Did I ever tell you that I once saw him, and shared your feeling of repulsion?"

"It was impossible to do the one without the other," returned Enfield. "And by the way, what an ass you must have thought me, not to know that this was a back way to Dr. Jekyll's! It was partly your own fault that I found it out, even when I did."

"So you found it out, did you?" said Utterson. "But if that be so, we may step into the court and take a look at the windows. To tell you the truth, I am uneasy about poor Jekyll; and even outside, I feel as if the presence of a friend might do him good."

The court was very cool and a little damp, and full of premature twilight, although the sky, high up overhead, was still bright with sunset. The middle one of the three windows was half-way open;

and sitting close beside it, taking the air with an infinite sadness of mien, like some disconsolate prisoner, Utterson saw Dr. Jekyll.

"What! Jekyll!" he cried. "I trust you are better."

"I am very low, Utterson," replied the doctor drearily, "very low. It will not last long, thank God."

"You stay too much indoors," said the lawyer. "You should be out, whipping up the circulation like Mr. Enfield and me. (This is my cousin—Mr. Enfield—Dr. Jekyll.) Come now; get your hat and take a quick turn with us."

"You are very good," sighed the other. "I should like to very much; but no, no, no, it is quite impossible; I dare not. But indeed, Utterson, I am very glad to see you; this is really a great pleasure; I would ask you and Mr. Enfield up, but the place is really not fit."

"Why, then," said the lawyer, good-naturedly, "the best thing we can do is to stay down here and speak with you from where we are."

"That is just what I was about to venture to propose," returned the doctor with a smile. But the words were hardly uttered, before the smile was struck out of his face and succeeded by an expression of such abject terror and despair, as froze the very blood of the two gentlemen below. They saw it but for a glimpse for the window was instantly thrust down; but that glimpse had been sufficient, and they turned and left the court without a word. In silence, too, they traversed the by-street; and it was not until they had come into a neighbouring thoroughfare, where even upon a Sunday there were still some stirrings of life, that Mr. Utterson at last turned and looked at his companion. They were both pale; and there was an answering horror in their eyes.

"God forgive us, God forgive us," said Mr. Utterson.

But Mr. Enfield only nodded his head very seriously, and walked on once more in silence.

The Last Night

MR. UTTERSON was sitting by his fireside one evening after dinner, when he was surprised to receive a visit from Poole.

"Bless me, Poole, what brings you here?" he cried; and then taking a second look at him, "What ails you?" he added; "is the doctor ill?"

"Mr. Utterson," said the man, "there is something wrong."

"Take a seat, and here is a glass of wine for you," said the lawyer. "Now, take your time, and tell me plainly what you want."

"You know the doctor's ways, sir," replied Poole, "and how he shuts himself up. Well, he's shut up again in the cabinet; and I don't like it, sir—I wish I may die if I like it. Mr. Utterson, sir, I'm afraid."

"Now, my good man," said the lawyer, "be explicit. What are you afraid of?"

"I've been afraid for about a week," returned Poole, doggedly disregarding the question, "and I can bear it no more."

The man's appearance amply bore out his words; his manner was altered for the worse; and except for the moment when he had first announced his terror, he had not once looked the lawyer in the face. Even now, he sat with the glass of wine untasted on his knee, and his eyes directed to a corner of the floor. "I can bear it no more," he repeated.

"Come," said the lawyer, "I see you have some good reason, Poole; I see there is something seriously amiss. Try to tell me what it is."

"I think there's been foul play," said Poole, hoarsely.

"Foul play!" cried the lawyer, a good deal frightened and rather inclined to be irritated in consequence. "What foul play! What does the man mean?"

"I daren't say, sir," was the answer; "but will you come along with me and see for yourself?"

Mr. Utterson's only answer was to rise and get his hat and greatcoat; but he observed with wonder the greatness of the relief that appeared upon the butler's face, and perhaps with no less, that the wine was still untasted when he set it down to follow.

It was a wild, cold, seasonable night of March, with a pale moon, lying on her back as though the wind had tilted her, and flying wrack of the most diaphanous and lawny texture. The wind made talking difficult, and flecked the blood into the face. It seemed to have swept the streets unusually bare of passengers, besides; for Mr. Utterson thought he had never seen that part of London so deserted. He could have wished it otherwise; never in his life had he been conscious of so sharp a wish to see and touch his fellow-creatures; for struggle as he might, there was borne in upon his mind a crushing anticipation of calamity. The square, when they got there, was full of wind and dust, and the thin trees in the garden were lashing themselves along the railing. Poole, who had kept all the way a pace or two ahead, now pulled up in the middle of the pavement, and in spite of the biting weather, took off his hat and mopped his brow with a red pocket-handkerchief. But for all the hurry of his coming, these were not the dews of exertion that he wiped away, but the moisture of some strangling anguish; for his face was white and his voice, when he spoke, harsh and broken.

"Well, sir," he said, "here we are, and God grant there be nothing wrong."

"Amen, Poole," said the lawyer.

Thereupon the servant knocked in a very guarded manner; the door was opened on the chain; and a voice asked from within, "Is that you, Poole?"

"It's all right," said Poole. "Open the door."

The hall, when they entered it, was brightly lighted up; the fire was built high; and about the hearth the whole of the servants, men and women, stood huddled together like a flock of sheep. At the sight of Mr. Utterson, the housemaid broke into hysterical whimpering; and the cook, crying out "Bless God! it's Mr. Utterson," ran forward as if to take him in her arms.

"What, what? Are you all here?" said the law-

yer peevishly. "Very irregular, very unseemly;
your master would be far from pleased."

"They're all afraid," said Poole.

Blank silence followed, no one protesting; only
the maid lifted her voice and now wept loudly.

"Hold your tongue!" Poole said to her, with a
ferocity of accent that testified to his own jangled
nerves; and indeed, when the girl had so suddenly raised the note of her lamentation, they had
all started and turned towards the inner door
with faces of dreadful expectation. "And now,"
continued the butler, addressing the knife-boy,
"reach me a candle, and we'll get this through
hands at once." And then he begged Mr. Utterson to follow him, and led the way to the back
garden.

"Now, sir," said he, "you come as gently as
you can. I want you to hear, and I don't want
you to be heard. And see here, sir, if by any
chance he was to ask you in, don't go."

Mr. Utterson's nerves, at this unlooked-for ter-
mination, gave a jerk that nearly threw him from
his balance; but he recollected his courage and
followed the butler into the laboratory building
through the surgical theatre, with its lumber of
crates and bottles, to the foot of the stair. Here
Poole motioned him to stand on one side and
listen; while he himself, setting down the candle
and making a great and obvious call on his reso-
lution, mounted the steps and knocked with a

somewhat uncertain hand on the red baize of the cabinet door.

"Mr. Utterson, sir, asking to see you," he called; and even as he did so, once more violently signed to the lawyer to give ear.

A voice answered from within: "Tell him I cannot see anyone," it said complainingly.

"Thank you, sir," said Poole, with a note of something like triumph in his voice; and taking up his candle, he led Mr. Utterson back across the yard and into the great kitchen, where the fire was out and the beetles were leaping on the floor.

"Sir," he said, looking Mr. Utterson in the eyes, "was that my master's voice?"

"It seems much changed," replied the lawyer, very pale, but giving look for look.

"Changed? Well, yes, I think so," said the butler. "Have I been twenty years in this man's house, to be deceived about his voice? No, sir; master's made away with; he was made away with eight days ago, when we heard him cry out upon the name of God; and *who's* in there instead of him, and *why* it stays there, is a thing that cries to Heaven, Mr. Utterson!"

"This is a very strange tale, Poole; this is rather a wild tale, my man," said Mr. Utterson, biting his finger. "Suppose it were as you suppose, supposing Dr. Jekyll to have been—well, murdered, what could induce the murderer to stay? That won't hold water; it doesn't commend itself to reason."

"Well, Mr. Utterson, you are a hard man to satisfy, but I'll do it yet," said Poole. "All this last week (you must know) him, or it, whatever it is that lives in that cabinet, has been crying night and day for some sort of medicine and cannot get it to his mind. It was sometimes his way—the master's, that is—to write his orders on a sheet of paper and throw it on the stair. We've had nothing else this week back; nothing but papers, and a closed door, and the very meals left there to be smuggled in when nobody was looking. Well, sir, every day, ay, and twice and thrice in the same day, there have been orders and complaints, and I have been sent flying to all the wholesale chemists in town. Every time I brought the stuff back, there would be another paper telling me to return it, because it was not pure, and another order to a different firm. This drug is wanted bitter bad, sir, whatever for."

"Have you any of these papers?" asked Mr. Utterson.

Poole felt in his pocket and handed out a crumpled note, which the lawyer, bending nearer to the candle, carefully examined. Its contents ran thus: "Dr. Jekyll presents his compliments to Messrs. Maw. He assures them that their last sample is impure and quite useless for his present purpose. In the year 18—, Dr. J. purchased a somewhat large quantity from Messrs. M. He now begs them to search with most sedulous care, and should any of the same quality be left, to forward it to him at once. Expense is no consideration. The importance of this to Dr. J. can hardly be exaggerated." So far the letter had run composedly enough, but here with a sudden splutter of the pen, the writer's emotion had broken loose. "For God's sake," he added, "find me some of the old."

"This is a strange note," said Mr. Utterson; and then sharply, "How do you come to have it open?"

"The man at Maw's was main angry, sir, and he threw it back to me like so much dirt," returned Poole.

"This is unquestionably the doctor's hand, do you know?" resumed the lawyer.

"I thought it looked like it," said the servant rather sulkily; and then, with another voice, "But what matters hand of write?" he said. "I've seen him!"

"Seen him?" repeated Mr. Utterson. "Well?"

"That's it!" said Poole. "It was this way. I came suddenly into the theatre from the garden. It seems he had slipped out to look for this drug or whatever it is; for the cabinet door was open, and there he was at the far end of the room digging among the crates. He looked up when I came in, gave a kind of cry, and whipped upstairs into the cabinet. It was but for one minute that I saw him, but the hair stood upon my head like quills. Sir, if that was my master, why had he a mask upon his face? If it was my master, why did he cry out like a rat, and run from me? I have served him long enough. And then . . ." The man paused and passed his hand over his face.

"These are all very strange circumstances," said Mr. Utterson, "but I think I begin to see daylight. Your master, Poole, is plainly seized with one of those maladies that both torture and deform the sufferer; hence, for aught I know, the alteration of his voice; hence the mask and the avoidance of his friends; hence his eagerness to find this drug, by means of which the poor soul retains some hope of ultimate recovery—God grant that he be not deceived! There is my explanation; it is sad enough, Poole, ay, and appalling to consider; but it is plain and natural, hangs well together, and delivers us from all exorbitant alarms."

"Sir," said the butler, turning to a sort of mottled pallor, "that thing was not my master, and there's the truth. My master"—here he looked round him and began to whisper—"is a tall, fine build of a man, and this was more of a dwarf." Utterson attempted to protest. "O, sir," cried Poole, "do you think I do not know my master after twenty years? Do you think I do not know where his head comes to in the cabinet door, where I saw him every morning of my life? No, sir, that thing in the mask was never Dr. Jekyll

—God knows what it was, but it was never Dr. Jekyll; and it is the belief of my heart that there was murder done."

"Poole," replied the lawyer, "if you say that, it will become my duty to make certain. Much as I desire to spare your master's feelings, much as I am puzzled by this note which seems to prove him to be still alive, I shall consider it my duty to break in that door."

"Ah, Mr. Utterson, that's talking!" cried the butler.

"And now comes the second question," resumed Utterson: "Who is going to do it?"

"Why, you and me, sir," was the undaunted reply.

"That's very well said," returned the lawyer; "and whatever comes of it, I shall make it my business to see you are no loser."

"There is an axe in the theatre," continued Poole; "and you might take the kitchen poker for yourself."

The lawyer took that rude but weighty instrument into his hand, and balanced it. "Do you know, Poole," he said, looking up, "that you and I are about to place ourselves in a position of some peril?"

"You may say so, sir, indeed," returned the butler.

"It is well, then, that we should be frank," said the other. "We both think more than we have said; let us make a clean breast. This masked figure that you saw, did you recognise it?"

"Well, sir, it went so quick, and the creature was so doubled up, that I could hardly swear to that," was the answer. "But if you mean, was it Mr. Hyde?—why, yes, I think it was! You see, it was much of the same bigness; and it had the same quick, light way with it; and then who else could have got in by the laboratory door? You have not forgot, sir, that at the time of the murder he had still the key with him? But that's not all. I don't know, Mr. Utterson, if you ever met this Mr. Hyde?"

"Yes," said the lawyer, "I once spoke with him."

"Then you must know as well as the rest of us that there was something queer about that gentleman—something that gave a man a turn—I don't know rightly how to say it, sir, beyond this: that you felt in your marrow kind of cold and thin."

"I own I felt something of what you describe," said Mr. Utterson.

"Quite so, sir," returned Poole. "Well, when that masked thing like a monkey jumped from among the chemicals and whipped into the cabinet, it went down my spine like ice. O, I know it's not evidence, Mr. Utterson; I'm book-learned enough for that; but a man has his feelings, and I give you my bible-word it was Mr. Hyde!"

"Ay, ay," said the lawyer. "My fears incline to the same point. Evil, I fear, founded—evil was sure to come—of that connection. Ay truly, I believe you; I believe poor Harry is killed; and I believe his murderer (for what purpose, God alone can tell) is still lurking in his victim's room. Well, let our name be vengeance. Call Bradshaw."

The footman came at the summons, very white and nervous.

"Put yourself together, Bradshaw," said the lawyer. "This suspense, I know, is telling upon all of you; but it is now our intention to make an end of it. Poole, here, and I are going to force our way into the cabinet. If all is well, my shoulders are broad enough to bear the blame. Meanwhile, lest anything should really be amiss, or any malefactor seek to escape by the back, you and the boy must go round the corner with a pair of good sticks and take your post at the laboratory door. We give you ten minutes, to get to your stations."

As Bradshaw left, the lawyer looked at his watch. "And now, Poole, let us get to ours," he said; and taking the poker under his arm, led the way into the yard. The scud had banked over the moon, and it was now quite dark. The wind, which only broke in puffs and draughts into that deep well of building, tossed the light of the candle to and fro about their steps, until they came into the shelter of the theatre, where they sat down silently to wait. London hummed solemnly all around; but nearer at hand, the stillness was only broken by the sounds of a footfall moving to and fro along the cabinet floor.

"So it will walk all day, sir," whispered Poole; "ay, and the better part of the night. Only when a new sample comes from the chemist, there's a bit of a break. Ah, it's an ill conscience that's such an enemy to rest! Ah, sir, there's blood foully shed in every step of it! But hark again, a little closer—put your heart in your ears, Mr. Utterson, and tell me, is that the doctor's foot?"

The steps fell lightly and oddly, with a certain swing, for all they went so slowly; it was different indeed from the heavy creaking tread of Henry Jekyll. Utterson sighed. "Is there never anything else?" he asked.

Poole nodded. "Once," he said. "Once I heard it weeping!"

"Weeping? how that?" said the lawyer, conscious of a sudden chill of horror.

"Weeping like a woman or a lost soul," said the butler. "I came away with that upon my heart, that I could have wept too."

But now the ten minutes drew to an end. Poole disinterred the axe from under a stack of packing straw; the candle was set upon the nearest table to light them to the attack; and they drew near with bated breath to where that patient foot was still going up and down, up and down, in the quiet of the night. "Jekyll," cried Utterson, with a loud voice, "I demand to see you." He paused a moment, but there came no reply. "I give you fair warning, our suspicions are aroused, and I must and shall see you," he resumed; "if not by fair means, then by foul—if not of your consent, then by brute force!"

"Utterson," said the voice, "for God's sake, have mercy!"

"Ah, that's not Jekyll's voice—it's Hyde's!" cried Utterson. "Down with the door, Poole!"

Poole swung the axe over his shoulder; the blow shook the building, and the red baize door leaped against the lock and hinges. A dismal screech, as of mere animal terror, rang from the cabinet. Up went the axe again, and again the panels crashed and the frame bounded; four times the blow fell; but the wood was tough and the fittings were of excellent workmanship; and it was not until the fifth, that the lock burst and the wreck of the door fell inwards on the carpet.

The besiegers, appalled by their own riot and the stillness that had succeeded, stood back a little and peered in. There lay the cabinet before their eyes in the quiet lamplight, a good fire glowing and chattering on the hearth, the kettle singing its thin strain, a drawer or two open, papers neatly set forth on the business table, and nearer the fire, the things laid out for tea; the quietest room, you would have said, and, but for the glazed presses full of chemicals, the most commonplace that night in London.

Right in the midst there lay the body of a man sorely contorted and still twitching. They drew near on tiptoe, turned it on its back and beheld the face of Edward Hyde. He was dressed in clothes far too large for him, clothes of the doctor's bigness; the cords of his face still moved with a semblance of life, but life was quite gone: and by the crushed phial in the hand and the strong smell of kernels that hung upon the air, Utterson knew that he was looking on the body of a self-destroyer.

"We have come too late," he said sternly, "whether to save or punish. Hyde is gone to his account; and it only remains for us to find the body of your master."

The far greater proportion of the building was occupied by the theatre, which filled almost the whole ground storey and was lighted from above, and by the cabinet, which formed an upper story at one end and looked upon the court. A corridor joined the theatre to the door on the by-street; and with this the cabinet communicated separately by a second flight of stairs. There were besides a few dark closets and a spacious cellar. All these they now thoroughly examined. Each closet needed but a glance, for all were empty, and all, by the dust that fell from their doors, had stood long unopened. The cellar, indeed, was filled with crazy lumber, mostly dating from the times of the surgeon who was Jekyll's predecessor; but even as they opened the door they were advertised of the uselessness of further search, by the fall of a perfect mat of cobweb which had for years sealed up the entrance. Nowhere was there any trace of Henry Jekyll, dead or alive.

Poole stamped on the flags of the corridor. "He must be buried here," he said, hearkening to the sound.

"Or he may have fled," said Utterson, and he turned to examine the door in the by-street. It was locked; and lying near by on the flags, they found the key, already stained with rust.

"This does not look like use," observed the lawyer.

"Use!" echoed Poole. "Do you not see, sir, it is broken? much as if a man had stamped on it."

"Ay," continued Utterson, "and the fractures, too, are rusty." The two men looked at each other with a scare. "This is beyond me, Poole," said the lawyer. "Let us go back to the cabinet."

They mounted the stair in silence, and still with an occasional awestruck glance at the dead body, proceeded more thoroughly to examine the contents of the cabinet. At one table, there were traces of chemical work, various measured heaps of some white salt being laid on glass saucers, as though for an experiment in which the unhappy man had been prevented.

"That is the same drug that I was always bringing him," said Poole; and even as he spoke, the kettle with a startling noise boiled over.

This brought them to the fireside, where the easychair was drawn cosily up, and the tea things stood ready to the sitter's elbow, the very sugar in the cup. There were several books on a shelf; one lay beside the tea things open, and Utterson was amazed to find it a copy of a pious work, for which Jekyll had several times expressed a great esteem, annotated, in his own hand, with startling blasphemies.

Next, in the course of their review of the chamber, the searchers came to the cheval-glass, into whose depths they looked with an involuntary horror. But it was so turned as to show them nothing but the rosy glow playing on the roof, the fire sparkling in a hundred repetitions along the glazed front of the presses, and their own pale and fearful countenances stooping to look in.

"This glass has seen some strange things, sir," whispered Poole.

"And surely none stranger than itself," echoed the lawyer in the same tones. "For what did Jekyll"—he caught himself up at the word with a start, and then conquering the weakness—"what could Jekyll want with it?" he said.

"You may say that!" said Poole.

Next they turned to the business table. On the desk, among the neat array of papers, a large envelope was uppermost, and bore, in the doctor's hand, the name of Mr. Utterson. The lawyer unsealed it, and several enclosures fell to the floor. The first was a will, drawn in the same eccentric terms as the one which he had returned six months before, to serve as a testament in case of death and as a deed of gift in case of disappearance; but in place of the name of Edward Hyde, the lawyer, with indescribable amazement, read the name of Gabriel John Utterson. He looked at Poole, and then back at the paper, and last of all at the dead malefactor stretched upon the carpet.

"My head goes round," he said. "He has been all these days in possession; he had no cause to like me; he must have raged to see himself displaced; and he has not destroyed this document."

He caught up the next paper; it was a brief note in the doctor's hand and dated at the top. "O Poole!" the lawyer cried, "he was alive and here this day. He cannot have been disposed of in so short a space; he must be still alive, he must have fled! And then, why fled? and how? and in that case, can we venture to declare this suicide? O, we must be careful. I foresee that we may yet involve your master in some dire catastrophe."

"Why don't you read it, sir?" asked Poole.

"Because I fear," replied the lawyer solemnly. God grant I have no cause for it!" And with that he brought the paper to his eyes and read as follows:

"My dear Utterson,—When this shall fall into your hands, I shall have disappeared, under what circumstances I have not the penetration to foresee, but my instinct and all the circumstances of my nameless situation tell me that the end is sure and must be early. Go then, and first read the narrative which Lanyon warned me he was to place in your hands; and if you care to hear more, turn to the confession of

"Your unworthy and unhappy friend,

"HENRY JEKYLL."

"There was a third enclosure?" asked Utterson.

"Here, sir," said Poole, and gave into his hands a considerable packet sealed in several places.

The lawyer put it in his pocket. "I would say nothing of this paper. If your master has fled or is dead, we may at least save his credit. It is now ten; I must go home and read these documents in quiet; but I shall be back before midnight, when we shall send for the police."

They went out, locking the door of the theatre behind them; and Utterson, once more leaving the servants gathered about the fire in the hall, trudged back to his office to read the two narratives in which this mystery was now to be explained.

Dr. Lanyon's Narrative

On the ninth of January, now four days ago, I received by the evening delivery a registered envelope, addressed in the hand of my colleague and old school companion, Henry Jekyll. I was a good deal surprised by this; for we were by no means in the habit of correspondence; I had seen the man, dined with him, indeed, the night before; and I could imagine nothing in our intercourse that should justify formality of registration. The contents increased my wonder; for this is how the letter ran:

"10th December, 18—.

"Dear Lanyon,—You are one of my oldest friends; and although we may have differed at times on scientific questions, I cannot remember, at least on my side, any break in our affection. There was never a day when, if you had said to me, 'Jekyll, my life, my honour, my reason, depend upon you,' I would not have sacrificed my left hand to help you. Lanyon, my life, my honour, my reason, are all at your mercy; if you fail me to-night, I am lost. You might suppose, after this preface, that I am going to ask you for something dishonourable to grant. Judge for yourself.

"I want you to postpone all other engagements

for to-night—ay, even if you were summoned to
the bedside of an emperor; to take a cab, unless
your carriage should be actually at the door; and
with this letter in your hand for consultation,
to drive straight to my house. Poole, my butler,
has his orders; you will find him waiting your
arrival with a locksmith. The door of my cabinet
is then to be forced: and you are to go in alone;
to open the glazed press (letter E) on the left
hand, breaking the lock if it be shut; and to
draw out, *with all its contents as they stand*, the
fourth drawer from the top or (which is the same
thing) the third from the bottom. In my extreme
distress of mind, I have a morbid fear of mis-
directing you; but even if I am in error, you
may know the right drawer by its contents: some
powders, a phial and a paper book. This drawer
I beg of you to carry back with you to Cavendish
Square exactly as it stands.

"That is the first part of the service: now for the
second. You should be back, if you set out at once
on the recipt of this, long before midnight; but
I will leave you that amount of margin, not only in
the fear of one of those obstacles that can neither
be prevented nor foreseen, but because an hour
when your servants are in bed is to be preferred
for what will then remain to do. At midnight, then,
I have to ask you to be alone in your consulting
room, to admit with your own hand into the house a
man who will present himself in my name, and to
place in his hands the drawer that you will have

brought with you from my cabinet. Then you will have played your part and earned my gratitude completely. Five minutes afterwards, if you insist upon an explanation, you will have understood that these arrangements are of capital importance; and that by the neglect of one of them, fantastic as they must appear, you might have charged your conscience with my death or the shipwreck of my reason.

"Confident as I am that you will not trifle with this appeal, my heart sinks and my hand trembles at the bare thought of such a possibility. Think of me at this hour, in a strange place, labouring under a blackness of distress that no fancy can exaggerate, and yet well aware that, if you will but punctually serve me, my troubles will roll away like a story that is told. Serve me, my dear Lanyon, and save

"Your friend,

"H. J.

"P.S.—I had already sealed this up when a fresh terror struck upon my soul. It is possible that the post-office may fail me, and this letter not come into your hands until to-morrow morning. In that case, dear Lanyon, do my errand when it shall be most convenient for you in the course of the day; and once more expect my messenger at midnight. It may then already be too late; and if that night passes without event, you will know that you have seen the last of Henry Jekyll."

Upon the reading of this letter, I made sure my colleague was insane; but till that was proved beyond the possibility of doubt, I felt bound to do as he requested. The less I understood of this farrago, the less I was in a position to judge of its importance; and an appeal so worded could not be set aside without a grave responsibility. I rose accordingly from table, got into a hansom, and drove straight to Jekyll's house. The butler was awaiting my arrival; he had received by the same post as mine a registered letter of instruction, and had sent at once for a locksmith and a carpenter. The tradesmen came while we were yet speaking; and we moved in a body to old Dr. Denman's surgical theatre, from which (as you are doubtless aware) Jekyll's private cabinet is most conveniently entered. The door was very strong, the lock excellent; the carpenter avowed he would have great trouble and have to do much damage, if force were to be used; and the locksmith was near despair. But this last was a handy fellow, and after two hours' work, the door stood open. The press marked E was unlocked; and I took out the drawer, had it filled up with straw and tied in a sheet, and returned with it to Cavendish Square.

Here I proceeded to examine its contents. The powders were neatly enough made up, but not with the nicety of the dispensing chemist; so that it was plain they were of Jekyll's private manufacture: and when I opened one of the wrappers I found what seemed to me a simple crystalline salt of a white colour. The phial, to which I next turned my attention, might have been about half full of a blood-red liquor, which was highly pungent to the sense of smell and seemed to me to contain phosphorus and some volatile ether. At the other ingredients I could make no guess. The book was an ordinary version book and contained little but a series of dates. These covered a period of many years, but I observed that the entries ceased nearly a year ago and quite abruptly. Here and there a brief remark was appended to a date, usually no more than a single word: "double" occurring perhaps six times in a total of several hundred entries; and once very early in the list and followed by several marks of exclamation, "total failure!!!" All this, though it whetted my curiosity, told me little that was definite. Here were a phial of some salt, and the record of a series of experiments that had led (like too many of Jekyll's investigations) to no end of practical usefulness. How could the presence of these articles in my house affect either the honour, the sanity, or the life of my flighty colleague? If his messenger could go to one place, why could he not go to another? And even granting some impediment, why was this gentleman to be received by me in secret? The more I reflected the more convinced I grew that I was dealing with a case of cerebral disease; and though I dismissed my servants to bed, I loaded an old revolver, that I might be found in some posture of self-defence.

Twelve o'clock had scarce rung out over London,
ere the knocker sounded very gently on the door.
I went myself at the summons, and found a small
man crouching against the pillars of the portico.

"Are you come from Dr. Jekyll?" I asked.

He told me "yes" by a constrained gesture; and
when I had bidden him enter, he did not obey me
without a searching backward glance into the darkness of the square. There was a policeman not far
off, advancing with his bull's eye open; and at the
sight, I thought my visitor started and made
greater haste.

These particulars struck me, I confess, disagreeably; and as I followed him into the bright light of
the consulting room, I kept my hand ready on my
weapon. Here, at last, I had a chance of clearly seeing him. I had never set eyes on him before, so
much was certain. He was small, as I have said;
I was struck besides with the shocking expression
of his face, with his remarkable combination of
great muscular activity and great apparent debility
of constitution, and—last but not least—with the
odd, subjective disturbance caused by his neighbourhood. This bore some resemblance to incip-
ient rigour, and was accompanied by a marked sink-
ing of the pulse. At the time, I set it down to
some idiosyncratic, personal distaste, and merely
wondered at the acuteness of the symptoms; but
I have since had reason to believe the cause to lie
much deeper in the nature of man, and to turn
on some nobler hinge than the principle of hatred.

This person (who had thus, from the first moment of his entrance, struck in me what I can only describe as a disgustful curiosity) was dressed in a fashion that would have made an ordinary person laughable; his clothes, that is to say, although they were of rich and sober fabric, were enormously too large for him in every measurement—the trousers hanging on his legs and rolled up to keep them from the ground, the waist of the coat below his haunches, and the collar sprawling wide upon his shoulders. Strange to relate, this ludicrous accoutrement was far from moving me to laughter. Rather, as there was something abnormal and misbegotten in the very essence of the creature that now faced me—something seizing, surprising and revolting—this fresh disparity seemed but to fit in with and to reinforce it; so that to my interest in the man's nature and character, there was added a curiosity as to his origin, his life, his fortune and status in the world.

These observations, though they have taken so great a space to be set down in, were yet the work of a few seconds. My visitor was, indeed, on fire with sombre excitement.

"Have you got it?" he cried. "Have you got it?" And so lively was his impatience that he even laid his hand upon my arm and sought to shake me.

I put him back, conscious at his touch of a certain icy pang along my blood. "Come, sir," said I. "You forget that I have not yet the pleasure of your acquaintance. Be seated, if you please." And

I showed him an example, and sat down myself
in my customary seat and with as fair an imita-
tion of my ordinary manner to a patient, as the
lateness of the hour, the nature of my preoccupa-
tions, and the horror I had of my visitor, would
suffer me to muster.

"I beg your pardon, Dr. Lanyon," he replied
civilly enough. "What you say is very well founded;
and my impatience has shown its heels to my politeness. I come here at the instance of your colleague, Dr. Henry Jekyll, on a piece of business
of some moment; and I understood . . ." He paused
and put his hand to his throat, and I could see, in
spite of his collected manner, that he was wrestling
against the approaches of the hysteria—"I understood, a drawer . . ."

But here I took pity on my visitor's suspense,
and some perhaps on my own growing curiosity.

"There it is, sir," said I, pointing to the drawer,
where it lay on the floor behind a table and still
covered with the sheet.

He sprang to it, and then paused, and laid his
hand upon his heart: I could hear his teeth grate
with the convulsive action of his jaws; and his face
was so ghastly to see that I grew alarmed both for
his life and reason.

"Compose yourself," said I.

He turned a dreadful smile to me, and as if
with the decision of despair, plucked away the
sheet. At sight of the contents, he uttered one loud
sob of such immense relief that I sat petrified. And

the next moment, in a voice that was already fairly well under control, "Have you a graduated glass?" he asked.

I rose from my place with something of an effort and gave him what he asked.

He thanked me with a smiling nod, measured out a few minims of the red tincture and added one of the powders. The mixture, which was at first of a reddish hue, began, in proportion as the crystals melted, to brighten in colour, to effervesce audibly, and to throw off small fumes of vapour. Suddenly and at the same moment, the ebullition ceased and the compound changed to a dark purple, which faded again more slowly to a watery green. My visitor, who had watched these metamorphoses with a keen eye, smiled, set down the glass upon the table, and then turned and looked upon me with an air of scrutiny.

"And now," said he, "to settle what remains. Will you be wise? will you be guided? will you suffer me to take this glass in my hand and to go forth from your house without further parley? or has the greed of curiosity too much command of you? Think before you answer, for it shall be done as you decide. As you decide, you shall be left as you were before, and neither richer nor wiser, unless the sense of service rendered to a man in mortal distress may be counted as a kind of riches of the soul. Or, if you shall so prefer to choose, a new province of knowledge and new avenues to fame and power shall be laid open to you, here, in this room, upon the instant; and your sight shall be blasted by a prodigy to stagger the unbelief of Satan."

"Sir," said I, affecting a coolness that I was far from truly possessing, "you speak enigmas, and you will perhaps not wonder that I hear you with no very strong impression of belief. But I have gone too far in the way of inexplicable services to pause before I see the end."

"It is well," replied my visitor. "Lanyon, you remember your vows: what follows is under the seal of our profession. And now, you who have so long been bound to the most narrow and material views, you who have denied the virtue of transcendental medicine, you who have derided your superiors—behold!"

He put the glass to his lips and drank at one gulp. A cry followed; he reeled, staggered, clutched at the table and held on, staring with injected eyes, gasping with open mouth; and as I looked there came, I thought, a change—he seemed to swell—his face became suddenly black and the features seemed to melt and alter—and the next moment, I had sprung to my feet and leaped back against the wall, my arm raised to shield me from that prodigy, my mind submerged in terror.

"O God!" I screamed, and "O God!" again and again; for there before my eyes—pale and shaken, and half fainting, and groping before him with his hands, like a man restored from death—there stood Henry Jekyll!

What he told me in the next hour, I cannot
bring my mind to set on paper. I saw what I saw,
I heard what I heard, and my soul sickened at it;
and yet now when that sight has faded from my
eyes, I ask myself if I believe it, and I cannot answer. My life is shaken to its roots; sleep has left
me; the deadliest terror sits by me at all hours of
the day and night; and I feel that my days are
numbered, and that I must die; and yet I shall die
incredulous. As for the moral turpitude that man
unveiled to me, even with tears of penitence, I cannot, even in memory, dwell on it without a start of
hórror. I will say but one thing, Utterson, and that
(if you can bring your mind to credit it) will be
more than enough. The creature who crept into my
house that night was, on Jekyll's own confession,
known by the name of Hyde and hunted for in
every corner of the land as the murderer of Carew.

HASTIE LANYON

Henry Jekyll's Full Statement
of the Case

I was born in the year 18— to a large fortune, endowed besides with excellent parts, inclined by nature to industry, fond of the respect of the wise and good among my fellowmen, and thus, as might have been supposed, with every guarantee of an honourable and distinguished future. And indeed the worst of my faults was a certain impatient gaiety of disposition, such as has made the happiness of many, but such as I found it hard to reconcile with my imperious desire to carry my head high, and wear a more than commonly grave countenance before the public. Hence it came about that I concealed my pleasures; and that when I reached years of reflection, and began to look round me and take stock of my progress and position in the world, I stood already committed to a profound duplicity of life. Many a man would have even blazoned such irregularities as I was guilty of; but from the high views that I had set before me, I regarded and hid them with an almost morbid sense of shame. It was thus rather the exacting nature of my aspirations than any particular degradation in my faults, that made me what I was, and, with even a deeper trench than in the majority of men, severed in me those provinces of good and ill which divide and compound man's dual nature. In this case, I was driven to reflect deeply and inveterately on that hard law of life, which lies at the root of religion and is one of the most plentiful springs of distress. Though so profound a double-dealer, I was in no sense a hypocrite; both sides of me were in dead earnest; I was no more myself when I laid aside restraint and plunged in shame, than when I laboured, in the eye of day, at the furtherance of knowledge or the relief of sorrow and suffering. And it chanced that the direction of my scientific studies, which led wholly towards the mystic and the transcendental, reacted and shed a strong light on this consciousness of the perennial war among my members. With every day, and from both sides of my intelligence, the moral and the intellectual, I thus drew steadily nearer to that truth, by whose partial discovery I have been doomed to such a dreadful shipwreck: that man is not truly one, but truly two. I say two, because the state of my own knowledge does not pass beyond that point. Others will follow, others will outstrip me on the same lines; and I hazard the guess that man will be ultimately known for a mere polity of multifarious, incongruous and independent denizens. I, for my part, from the nature of my life, advanced infallibly in one direction and in one direction only. It was on the moral side, and in my own person, that I learned to recognise the thorough and primitive duality of man; I saw that, of the two natures that contended in the field

of my consciousness, even if I could rightly be said
to be either, it was only because I was radically
both; and from an early date, even before the
course of my scientific discoveries had begun to
suggest the most naked possibility of such a miracle, I had learned to dwell with pleasure, as a beloved daydream, on the thought of the separation
of these elements. If each, I told myself, could
be housed in separate identities, life would be relieved of all that was unbearable; the unjust might
go his way, delivered from the aspirations and remorse of his more upright twin; and the just could
walk steadfastly and securely on his upward path,
doing the good things in which he found his pleasure, and no longer exposed to disgrace and penitence by the hands of this extraneous evil. It was
the curse of mankind that these incongruous fag-
gots were thus bound together—that in the agonised
womb of consciousness, these polar twins should
be continuously struggling. How, then, were they
dissociated?

I was so far in my reflections when, as I have
said, a side light began to shine upon the subject
from the laboratory table. I began to perceive more
deeply than it has ever yet been stated, the trembling immateriality, the mistlike transience, of this
seemingly so solid body in which we walk attired.
Certain agents I found to have the power to shake
and pluck back that fleshly vestment, even as a
wind might toss the curtains of a pavilion. For two
good reasons, I will not enter deeply into this scien-

tific branch of my confession. First, because I have
been made to learn that the doom and burthen of
our life is bound for ever on man's shoulders, and
when the attempt is made to cast it off, it but returns upon us with more unfamiliar and more aw-
ful pressure. Second, because, as my narrative will
make, alas! too evident, my discoveries were incom-
plete. Enough then, that I not only recognised
my natural body from the mere aura and effulgence
of certain of the powers that made up my spirit,
but managed to compound a drug by which these
powers should be dethroned from their supremacy,
and a second form and countenance substituted,
none the less natural to me because they were the
expression, and bore the stamp of lower elements
in my soul.

I hesitated long before I put this theory to the
test of practice. I knew well that I risked death;
for any drug that so potently controlled and shook
the very fortress of identity, might, by the least
scruple of an overdose or at the least inopportunity
in the moment of exhibition, utterly blot out that
immaterial tabernacle which I looked to it to
change. But the temptation of a discovery so singular and profound at last overcame the sugges-
tions of alarm. I had long since prepared my
tincture; I purchased at once, from a firm of wholesale chemists, a large quantity of a particular salt
which I knew, from my experiments, to be the last
ingredient required; and late one accursed night,
I compounded the elements, watched them boil

and smoke together in the glass, and when the
ebullition had subsided, with a strong glow of courage, drank off the potion.

The most racking pangs succeeded: a grinding
in the bones, deadly nausea, and a horror of the
spirit that cannot be exceeded at the hour of birth
or death. Then these agonies began swiftly to subside, and I came to myself as if out of a great
sickness. There was something strange in my sensations, something indescribably new and, from its
very novelty, incredibly sweet. I felt younger,
lighter, happier in body; within I was conscious
of a heady recklessness, a current of disordered
sensual images running like a millrace in my fancy,
a solution of the bonds of obligation, an unknown
but not an innocent freedom of the soul. I knew
myself, at the first breath of this new life, to be
more wicked, tenfold more wicked, sold a slave
to my original evil; and the thought, in that moment, braced and delighted me like wine.
I stretched out my hands, exulting in the freshness
of these sensations; and in the act, I was suddenly
aware that I had lost in stature.

There was no mirror, at that date, in my room;
that which stands beside me as I write, was brought
there later on and for the very purpose of these
transformations. The night, however, was far
gone into the morning—the morning, black as it
was, was nearly ripe for the conception of the
day—the inmates of my house were locked in the
most rigorous hours of slumber; and I determined,

flushed as I was with hope and triumph, to venture
in my new shape as far as to my bedroom. I
crossed the yard, wherein the constellations looked
down upon me, I could have thought, with wonder, the first creature of that sort that their unsleep-
ing vigilance had yet disclosed to them; I stole
through the corridors, a stranger in my own house;
and coming to my room, I saw for the first time
the appearance of Edward Hyde.

I must here speak by theory alone, saying not
that which I know, but that which I suppose to
be most probable. The evil side of my nature, to
which I had now transferred the stamping efficacy,
was less robust and less developed than the good
which I had just deposed. Again, in the course of
my life, which had been, after all, nine tenths a
life of effort, virtue and control, it had been much
less exercised and much less exhausted. And hence,
as I think, it came about that Edward Hyde was
so much smaller, slighter and younger than Henry
Jekyll. Even as good shone upon the countenance
of the one, evil was written broadly and plainly on
the face of the other. Evil besides (which I must
still believe to be the lethal side of man) had left
on that body an imprint of deformity and decay.
And yet when I looked upon that ugly idol in the
glass, I was conscious of no repugnance, rather
of a leap of welcome. This, too, was myself. It
seemed natural and human. In my eyes it bore
a livelier image of the spirit, it seemed more express and single, than the imperfect and divided

countenance I had been hitherto accustomed to call mine. And in so far I was doubtless right. I have observed that when I wore the semblance of Edward Hyde, none could come near to me at first without a visible misgiving of the flesh. This, as I take it, was because all human beings, as we meet them, are commingled out of good and evil: and Edward Hyde, alone in the ranks of mankind, was pure evil.

I lingered but a moment at the mirror: the second and conclusive experiment had yet to be attempted; it yet remained to be seen if I had lost my identity beyond redemption and must flee before daylight from a house that was no longer mine; and hurrying back to my cabinet, I once more prepared and drank the cup, once more suffered the pangs of dissolution, and came to myself once more with the character, the stature and the face of Henry Jekyll.

That night I had come to the fatal cross-roads. Had I approached my discovery in a more noble spirit, had I risked the experiment while under the empire of generous or pious aspirations, all must have been otherwise, and from these agonies of death and birth, I had come forth an angel instead of a fiend. The drug had no discriminating action; it was neither diabolical nor divine; it but shook the doors of the prisonhouse of my disposition; and like the captives of Philippi, that which stood within ran forth. At that time my virtue slumbered; my evil, kept awake by ambition, was alert and swift to seize the occasion; and the thing that was projected was Edward Hyde. Hence, although I had now two characters as well as two appearances, one was wholly evil, and the other was still the old Henry Jekyll, that incongruous compound of whose reformation and improvement I had already learned to despair. The movement was thus wholly toward the worse.

Even at that time, I had not conquered my aversions to the dryness of a life of study. I would still be merrily disposed at times; and as my pleasures were (to say the least) undignified, and I was not only well known and highly considered, but growing towards the elderly man, this incoherency of my life was daily growing more unwelcome. It was on this side that my new power tempted me until I fell in slavery. I had but to drink the cup, to doff at once the body of the noted professor, and to assume, like a thick cloak, that of Edward Hyde. I smiled at the notion; it seemed to me at the time to be humourous; and I made my preparations with the most studious care. I took and furnished that house in Soho, to which Hyde was tracked by the police; and engaged as a housekeeper a creature whom I knew well to be silent and unscrupulous. On the other side, I announced to my servants that a Mr. Hyde (whom I described) was to have full liberty and power about my house in the square; and to parry mishaps, I even called and made myself a familiar object, in my second character. I next drew up that will to which you

so much objected; so that if anything befell me in
the person of Dr. Jekyll, I could enter on that of
Edward Hyde without pecuniary loss. And thus
fortified, as I supposed, on every side, I began to
profit by the strange immunities of my position.

Men have before hired bravos to transact their
crimes, while their own person and reputation sat
under shelter. I was the first that ever did so for
his pleasures. I was the first that could plod in
the public eye with a load of genial respectability,
and in a moment, like a schoolboy, strip off these
lendings and spring headlong into the sea of liberty. But for me, in my impenetrable mantle, the
safety was complete. Think of it—I did not even
exist! Let me but escape into my laboratory door,
give me but a second or two to mix and swallow
the draught that I had always standing ready; and
whatever he had done, Edward Hyde would pass
away like the stain of breath upon a mirror; and
there in his stead, quietly at home, trimming the
midnight lamp in his study, a man who could af-
ford to laugh at suspicion, would be Henry Jekyll.

The pleasures which I made haste to seek in
my disguise were, as I have said, undignified; I
would scarce use a harder term. But in the hands
of Edward Hyde, they soon began to turn toward
the monstrous. When I would come back from these
excursions, I was often plunged into a kind of wonder at my vicarious depravity. This familiar that
I called out of my own soul, and sent forth alone
to do his good pleasure, was a being inherently

malign and villainous; his every act and thought
centered on self; drinking pleasure with bestial
avidity from any degree of torture to another; re-
lentless like a man of stone. Henry Jekyll stood
at times aghast before the acts of Edward Hyde;
but the situation was apart from ordinary laws, and
insidiously relaxed the grasp of conscience. It was
Hyde, after all, and Hyde alone, that was guilty.
Jekyll was no worse; he woke again to his good
qualities seemingly unimpaired; he would even
make haste, where it was possible, to undo the
evil done by Hyde. And thus his conscience slumbered.

Into the details of the infamy at which I thus
connived (for even now I can scarce grant that I
committed it) I have no design of entering; I mean
but to point out the warnings and the successive
steps with which my chastisement approached. I
met with one accident which, as it brought on no
consequence, I shall no more than mention. An act
of cruelty to a child aroused against me the anger
of a passer-by, whom I recognised the other day
in the person of your kinsman; the doctor and
the child's family joined him; there were moments
when I feared for my life; and at last, in order to
pacify their too just resentment, Edward Hyde had
to bring them to the door, and pay them in a
cheque drawn in the name of Henry Jekyll. But
this danger was easily eliminated from the future,
by opening an account at another bank in the name
of Edward Hyde himself; and when, by sloping

my own hand backward, I had supplied my double
with a signature, I thought I sat beyond the reach
of fate.

Some two months before the murder of Sir Danvers, I had been out for one of my adventures, had
returned at a late hour, and woke the next day in
bed with somewhat odd sensations. It was in vain
I looked about me; in vain I saw the decent furni-
ture and tall proportions of my room in the square;
in vain that I recognised the pattern of the bed
curtains and the design of the mahogany frame;
something still kept insisting that I was not where
I was, that I had not wakened where I seemed to
be, but in the little room in Soho where I was
accustomed to sleep in the body of Edward Hyde.
I smiled to myself, and, in my psychological way,
began lazily to inquire into the elements of this
illusion, occasionally, even as I did so, dropping
back into a comfortable morning doze. I was still
so engaged when, in one of my more wakeful moments, my eyes fell upon my hand. Now the hand
of Henry Jekyll (as you have often remarked) was
professional in shape and size: it was large, firm,
white and comely. But the hand which I now saw,
clearly enough, in the yellow light of a mid-Lon-
don morning, lying half shut on the bedclothes,
was lean, corded, knuckly, of a dusky pallor and
thickly shaded with a swart growth of hair. It was
the hand of Edward Hyde.

I must have stared upon it for near half a minute, sunk as I was in the mere stupidity of wonder,

before terror woke up in my breast as sudden and
startling as the crash of cymbals; and bounding
from my bed, I rushed to the mirror. At the sight
that met my eyes, my blood was changed into something exquisitely thin and icy. Yes, I had gone to
bed Henry Jekyll, I had awakened Edward Hyde.
How was this to be explained? I asked myself; and
then, with another bound of terror—how was it to
be remedied? It was well on in the morning; the
servants were up; all my drugs were in the cabinet—a long journey down two pairs of stairs,
through the back passage, across the open court
and through the anatomical theatre, from where I
was then standing horror-struck. It might indeed
be possible to cover my face; but of what use was
that, when I was unable to conceal the alteration
in my stature? And then with an overpowering
sweetness of relief, it came back upon my mind
that the servants were already used to the coming
and going of my second self. I had soon dressed,
as well as I was able, in clothes of my own size:
had soon passed through the house, where Bradshaw stared and drew back at seeing Mr. Hyde at
such an hour and in such a strange array; and
ten minutes later, Dr. Jekyll had returned to his
own shape and was sitting down, with a darkened
brow, to make a feint of breakfasting.

Small indeed was my appetite. This inexplicable
incident, this reversal of my previous experience,
seemed, like the Babylonian finger on the wall, to
be spelling out the letters of my judgment; and

I began to reflect more seriously than ever before
on the issues and possibilities of my double existence. That part of me which I had the power of
projecting, had lately been much exercised and
nourished; it had seemed to me of late as though
the body of Edward Hyde had grown in stature,
as though (when I wore that form) I were conscious of a more generous tide of blood; and I
began to spy a danger that, if this were much prolonged, the balance of my nature might be perma-
nently overthrown, the power of voluntary change
be forfeited, and the character of Edward Hyde
become irrevocably mine. The power of the drug
had not been always equally displayed. Once, very
early in my career, it had totally failed me; since
then I had been obliged on more than one occasion to double, and once, with infinite risk of death,
to treble the amount; and these rare uncertainties
had cast hitherto the sole shadow on my content-
ment. Now, however, and in the light of that morning's accident, I was led to remark that whereas,
in the beginning, the difficulty had been to throw
off the body of Jekyll, it had of late gradually
but decidedly transferred itself to the other side.
All things therefore seemed to point to this; that I
was slowly losing hold of my original and better
self, and becoming slowly incorporated with my
second and worse.

Between these two, I now felt I had to choose.
My two natures had memory in common, but all
other faculties were most unequally shared be-

tween them. Jekyll (who was composite) now with
the most sensitive apprehensions, now with a
greedy gusto, projected and shared in the pleasures
and adventures of Hyde; but Hyde was indifferent
to Jekyll, or but remembered him as the mountain
bandit remembers the cavern in which he conceals
himself from pursuit. Jekyll had more than a
father's interest; Hyde had more than a son's in-
difference. To cast in my lot with Jekyll, was to
die to those appetites which I had long secretly
indulged and had of late begun to pamper. To
cast it in with Hyde, was to die to a thousand in-
terests and aspirations, and to become, at a blow
and forever, despised and friendless. The bargain
might appear unequal; but there was still another
consideration in the scales; for while Jekyll would
suffer smartingly in the fires of abstinence, Hyde
would be not even conscious of all that he had lost.
Strange as my circumstances were, the terms of
this debate are as old and commonplace as man;
much the same inducements and alarms cast the
die for any tempted and trembling sinner; and it
fell out with me, as it falls with so vast a majority of my fellows, that I chose the better part
and was found wanting in the strength to keep
to it.

Yes, I preferred the elderly and discontented doctor, surrounded by friends and cherishing honest
hopes; and bade a resolute farewell to the liberty,
the comparative youth, the light step, leaping impulses and secret pleasures, that I had enjoyed in

the disguise of Hyde. I made this choice perhaps
with some unconscious reservation, for I neither
gave up the house in Soho, nor destroyed the
clothes of Edward Hyde, which still lay ready in
my cabinet. For two months, however, I was true
to my determination; for two months, I led a life
of such severity as I had never before attained
to, and enjoyed the compensations of an approving
conscience. But time began at last to obliterate
the freshness of my alarm; the praises of conscience
began to grow into a thing of course; I began to
be tortured with throes and longings, as of Hyde
struggling after freedom; and at last, in an hour
of moral weakness, I once again compounded and
swallowed the transforming draught.

I do not suppose that, when a drunkard reasons
with himself upon his vice, he is once out of five
hundred times affected by the dangers that he runs
through his brutish, physical insensibility; neither
had I, long as I had considered my position, made
enough allowance for the complete moral insensibility and insensate readiness to evil, which were
the leading characters of Edward Hyde. Yet it was
by these that I was punished. My devil had been
long caged, he came out roaring. I was conscious,
even when I took the draught, of a more unbridled,
a more furious propensity to ill. It must have been
this, I suppose, that stirred in my soul that tempest
of impatience with which I listened to the civilities
of my unhappy victim; I declare, at least, before
God, no man morally sane could have been guilty

of that crime upon so pitiful a provocation; and that I struck in no more reasonable spirit than that in which a sick child may break a plaything. But I had voluntarily stripped myself of all those balancing instincts by which even the worst of us continues to walk with some degree of steadiness among temptations; and in my case, to be tempted, however slightly, was to fall.

Instantly the spirit of hell awoke in me and raged. With a transport of glee, I mauled the unresisting body, tasting delight from every blow; and it was not till weariness had begun to succeed, that I was suddenly, in the top fit of my delirium, struck through the heart by a cold thrill of terror. A mist dispersed; I saw my life to be forfeit; and fled from the scene of these excesses, at once glorying and trembling, my lust of evil gratified and stimulated, my love of life screwed to the topmost peg. I ran to the house in Soho, and (to make assurance doubly sure) destroyed my papers; thence I set out through the lamplit streets, in the same divided ecstasy of mind, gloating on my crime, light-headedly devising others in the future, and yet still hastening and still hearkening in my wake for the steps of the avenger. Hyde had a song upon his lips as he compounded the draught, and as he drank it, pledged the dead man. The pangs of transformation had not done tearing him, before Henry Jekyll, with streaming tears of gratitude and remorse, had fallen upon his knees and lifted his clasped hands to God. The veil of self-indulgence was rent from head to foot. I saw my life as a whole: I followed it up from the days of childhood, when I had walked with my father's hand, and through the self-denying toils of my professional life, to arrive again and again, with the same sense of unreality, at the damned horrors of the evening. I could have screamed aloud; I sought with tears and prayers to smother down the crowd of hideous images and sounds with which my memory swarmed against me; and still, between the petitions, the ugly face of my iniquity stared into my soul. As the acuteness of this remorse began to die away, it was succeeded by a sense of joy. The problem of my conduct was solved. Hyde was thenceforth impossible; whether I would or not, I was now confined to the better part of my existence; and O, how I rejoiced to think of it! with what willing humility I embraced anew the restrictions of natural life! with what sincere renunciation I locked the door by which I had so often gone and come, and ground the key under my heel!

The next day, came the news that the murder had been overlooked, that the guilt of Hyde was patent to the world, and that the victim was a man high in public estimation. It was not only a crime, it had been a tragic folly. I think I was glad to know it; I think I was glad to have my better impulses thus buttressed and guarded by the terrors of the scaffold. Jekyll was now my city of refuge; let but Hyde peep out an instant, and the hands of all men would be raised to take and slay him.

I resolved in my future conduct to redeem the past; and I can say with honesty that my resolve was fruitful of some good. You know yourself how earnestly, in the last months of the last year, I laboured to relieve suffering; you know that much was done for others, and that the days passed quietly, almost happily for myself. Nor can I truly say that I wearied of this beneficent and innocent life; I think instead that I daily enjoyed it more completely; but I was still cursed with my duality of purpose; and as the first edge of my penitence wore off, the lower side of me, so long indulged, so recently chained down, began to growl for licence. Not that I dreamed of resuscitating Hyde; the bare idea of that would startle me to frenzy: no, it was in my own person that I was once more tempted to trifle with my conscience; and it was as an ordinary secret sinner that I at last fell before the assualts of temptation.

There comes an end to all things; the most capacious measure is filled at last; and this brief condescension to my evil finally destroyed the balance of my soul. And yet I was not alarmed; the fall seemed natural, like a return to the old days before I had made my discovery. It was a fine, clear, January day, wet under foot where the frost had melted, but cloudless overhead; and the Regent's Park was full of winter chirrupings and sweet with spring odours. I sat in the sun on a bench; the animal within me licking the chops of memory; the spiritual side a little drowsed, prom-

ising subsequent penitence, but not yet moved to
begin. After all, I reflected, I was like my neigh-
bours; and then I smiled, comparing myself with
other men, comparing my active good-will with the
lazy cruelty of their neglect. And at the very moment of that vainglorious thought, a qualm came
over me, a horrid nausea and the most deadly shud-
ering. These passed away, and left me faint; and
then as in its turn faintness subsided, I began to be
aware of a change in the temper of my thoughts, a
greater boldness, a contempt of danger, a solution
of the bonds of obligation. I looked down; my
clothes hung formlessly on my shrunken limbs;
the hand that lay on my knee was corded and hairy.
I was once more Edward Hyde. A moment before
I had been safe of all men's respect, wealthy, beloved—the cloth laying for me in the dining-room at
home; and now I was the common quarry of mankind, hunted, houseless, a known murderer, thrall
to the gallows.

My reason wavered, but it did not fail me utterly. I have more than once observed that, in my
second character, my faculties seemed sharpened
to a point and my spirits more tensely elastic; thus
it came about that, where Jekyll perhaps might
have succumbed, Hyde rose to the importance of
the moment. My drugs were in one of the presses
of my cabinet; how was I to reach them? That was
the problem that (crushing my temples in my
hands) I set myself to solve. The laboratory door
I had closed. If I sought to enter by the house, my

own servants would consign me to the gallows. I saw I must employ another hand, and thought of Lanyon. How was he to be reached? how persuaded? Supposing that I escaped capture in the streets, how was I to make my way into his presence? and how should I, an unknown and displeasing visitor, prevail on the famous physician to rifle the study of his colleague, Dr. Jekyll? Then I remembered that of my original character, one part remained to me: I could write my own hand; and once I had conceived that kindling spark, the way that I must follow became lighted up from end to end.

Thereupon, I arranged my clothes as best I could, and summoning a passing hansom, drove to an hotel in Portland Street, the name of which I chanced to remember. At my appearance (which was indeed comical enough, however tragic a fate these garments covered) the driver could not conceal his mirth. I gnashed my teeth upon him with a gust of devilish fury; and the smile withered from his face—happily for him—yet more happily for myself, for in another instant I had certainly dragged him from his perch. At the inn, as I entered, I looked about me with so black a countenance as made the attendants tremble; not a look did they exchange in my presence; but obsequiously took my orders, led me to a private room, and brought me wherewithal to write. Hyde in danger of his life was a creature new to me; shaken with inordinate anger, strung to the pitch of murder, lust-

ing to inflict pain. Yet the creature was astute;
mastered his fury with a great effort of the will;
composed his two important letters, one to Lanyon
and one to Poole; and that he might receive actual
evidence of their being posted, sent them out with
directions that they should be registered. Thence-
forward, he sat all day over the fire in the private
room, gnawing his nails; there he dined, sitting
alone with his fears, the waiter visibly quailing before his eye; and thence, when the night was fully
come, he set forth in the corner of a closed cab,
and was driven to and fro about the streets of the
city. He, I say—I cannot say, I. That child of Hell
had nothing human; nothing lived in him but fear
and hatred. And when at last, thinking the driver
had begun to grow suspicious, he discharged the
cab and ventured on foot, attired in his misfitting
clothes, an object marked out for observation, into
the midst of the nocturnal passengers, these two
base passions raged within him like a tempest. He
walked fast, hunted by his fears, chattering to himself, skulking through the less frequented thor-
oughfares, counting the minutes that still divided
him from midnight. Once a woman spoke to him,
offering, I think, a box of lights. He smote her in
the face, and she fled.

When I came to myself at Lanyon's, the horror
of my old friend perhaps affected me somewhat: I
do not know; it was at least but a drop in the sea
to the abhorrence with which I looked back upon
these hours. A change had come over me. It was

no longer the fear of the gallows, it was the horror of being Hyde that racked me. I received Lanyon's condemnation partly in a dream; it was partly in a dream that I came home to my own house and got into bed. I slept after the prostration of the day, with a stringent and profound slumber which not even the nightmares that wrung me could avail to break. I awoke in the morning shaken, weakened, but refreshed. I still hated and feared the thought of the brute that slept within me, and I had not of course forgotten the appalling dangers of the day before; but I was once more at home, in my own house and close to my drugs; and gratitude for my escape shone so strong in my soul that it almost rivalled the brightness of hope.

I was stepping leisurely across the court after breakfast, drinking the chill of the air with pleasure, when I was seized again with those indescribable sensations that heralded the change; and I had but the time to gain the shelter of my cabinet, before I was once again raging and freezing with the passions of Hyde. It took on this occasion a double dose to recall me to myself; and alas! six hours after, as I sat looking sadly in the fire, the pangs returned, and the drug had to be re-administered. In short, from that day forth it seemed only by a great effort as of gymnastics, and only under the immediate stimulation of the drug, that I was able to wear the countenance of Jekyll. At all hours of the day and night, I would be taken with the premonitory shudder; above all, if I slept, or even

dozed for a moment in my chair, it was always as
Hyde that I awakened. Under the strain of this
continually impending doom and by the sleepless-
ness to which I now condemned myself, ay, even
beyond what I had thought possible to man, I became, in my own person, a creature eaten up and
emptied by fever, languidly weak both in body and
mind, and solely occupied by one thought: the
horror of my other self. But when I slept, or when
the virtue of the medicine wore off, I would leap
almost without transition (for the pangs of transformation grew daily less marked) into the possession of a fancy brimming with images of terror,
a soul boiling with causeless hatreds, and a body
that seemed not strong enough to contain the raging energies of life. The powers of Hyde seemed
to have grown with the sickliness of Jekyll. And
certainly the hate that now divided them was equal
on each side. With Jekyll, it was a thing of vital
instinct. He had now seen the full deformity of
that creature that shared with him some of the
phenomena of consciousness, and was co-heir with
him to death: and beyond these links of commu-
nity, which in themselves made the most poignant
part of his distress, he thought of Hyde, for all his
energy of life, as of something not only hellish but
inorganic. This was the shocking thing; that the
slime of the pit seemed to utter cries and voices;
that the amorphous dust gesticulated and sinned;
that what was dead, and had no shape, should
usurp the offices of life. And this again, that that

insurgent horror was knit to him closer than a wife,
closer than an eye; lay caged in his flesh, where
he heard it mutter and felt it struggle to be born;
and at every hour of weakness, and in the confidence of slumber, prevailed against him, and
deposed him out of life. The hatred of Hyde for
Jekyll was of a different order. His terror of the
gallows drove him continually to commit tempo-
rary suicide, and return to his subordinate station
of a part instead of a person; but he loathed the
necessity, he loathed the despondency into which
Jekyll was now fallen, and he resented the dislike
with which he was himself regarded. Hence the
ape-like tricks that he would play me, scrawling in
my own hand blasphemies on the pages of my
books, burning the letters and destroying the portrait of my father; and indeed, had it not been for
his fear of death, he would long ago have ruined
himself in order to involve me in the ruin. But his
love of life is wonderful; I go further: I, who sicken
and freeze at the mere thought of him, when I
recall the abjection and passion of this attach-
ment, and when I know how he fears my power to
cut him off by suicide, I find it in my heart to pity
him.

It is useless, and the time awfully fails me, to
prolong this description; no one has ever suffered
such torments, let that suffice; and yet even to
these, habit brought—no, not alleviation—but a certain callousness of soul, a certain acquiescence of
despair; and my punishment might have gone on

for years, but for the last calamity which has now fallen, and which has finally severed me from my own face ånd nature. My provision of the salt, which had never been renewed since the date of the first experiment, began to run low. I sent out for a fresh supply and mixed the draught; the ebullition followed, and the first change of colour, not the second; I drank it and it was without efficiency. You will learn from Poole how I have had London ransacked; it was in vain; and I am now persuaded that my first supply was impure, and that it was that unknown impurity which lent efficacy to the draught.

About a week has passed, and I am now finishing this statement under the influence of the last of the old powders. This, then, is the last time, short of a miracle, that Henry Jekyll can think his own thoughts or see his own face (now how sadly altered!) in the glass. Nor must I delay too long to bring my writing to an end; for if my narrative has hitherto escaped destruction, it has been by a combination of great prudence and great good luck. Should the throes of change take me in the act of writing it, Hyde will tear it in pieces; but if some time shall have elapsed after I have laid it by, his wonderful selfishness and circumscription to the moment will probably save it once again from the action of his ape-like spite. And indeed the doom that is closing on us both has already changed and crushed him. Half an hour from now, when I shall again and forever reindue that hated personality, I

know how I shall sit shuddering and weeping in
my chair, or continue, with the most strained and
fearstruck ecstasy of listening, to pace up and down
this room (my last earthly refuge) and give ear to
every sound of menace. Will Hyde die upon the
scaffold? or will he find courage to release himself
at the last moment? God knows; I am careless; this
is my true hour of death, and what is to follow
concerns another than myself. Here then, as I lay
down the pen and proceed to seal up my confession, I bring the life of that unhappy Henry Jekyll
to an end.

Afterword:

Who is Hyde?

by Jerome Charyn

1.

Dr. Jekyll and Mr. Hyde would be a laughable little circus of a book, in which a "smooth-faced" doctor of fifty drinks from a magic bottle and changes into a murderous monkey man, were it not for Edward Hyde. Hyde is too forceful a character, too complex, to be imprisoned inside a crude case of split personalities. He won't be part of anybody's little circus, even though Jekyll tries to reduce him into an easy formula of everything that is foul in his own nature: "I had learned to dwell with pleasure, as a beloved daydream, on the thought of the separation of these elements [good and evil]. If each, I told myself, could be housed in separate identities, life would be relieved of all that was unbearable; the unjust might go his way, delivered from the aspirations and remorse of his more upright twin; and the just could walk steadfastly and securely on his upward path."

But Hyde also exists outside of Jekyll's dream. He has an energy, a will to be alive, that doesn't fit so readily into the novel's dualistic scheme. Who is

Hyde? We glimpse at him through the eyes of Jekyll's lawyer, Gabriel John Utterson of Gaunt Street, a man who never smiles. The lawyer is "lean, long, dusty." Hyde becomes a terrifying threat to Utterson's rigid way of life. After he learns that the mysterious Mr. Hyde has trampled on a little girl, the "figure" of Hyde "haunted the lawyer all night; and if at any time he dozed over, it was but to see it glide more stealthily through sleeping houses, or move the more swiftly and still the more swiftly, even to dizziness, through wider labyrinths of lamplighted city, and at every street corner crush a child and leave her screaming. And still the figure had no face by which he might know it; even in his dreams, it had no face."

Utterson cannot allow Hyde to have a face. Hyde is a troglodyte for him, an underground creature, "hardly human." "Pale and dwarfish," Hyde gave "an impression of deformity without any nameable malformation." Utterson returns to this vague "unexpressed deformity" several times, as if it were a metaphysical scar that has invaded *all* of Hyde. The dry lawyer cannot reconcile his own secret wish to explode, to convert his lean, long, dusty self into some forbidden energy. So Hyde becomes that unnameable thing, "troglodytic," without a face.

But Hyde does have a face, and we can move a bit closer to it by turning to Robert Louis Stevenson. Stevenson was tubercular during most of his adult life, a kind of invalid. "*Dr. Jekyll and Mr. Hyde* was written in bed, at Bournemouth on the English Channel, in 1885 in between hemorrhages from the lungs," as Vladimir Nabokov tells us in his *Lectures on Literature*. Hard up for money, feverish, he began the story of Jekyll and Hyde after coming out of a bad dream. Stevenson was a pale, sickly rebel who had defied his father, an industrious civil engineer. He chased after a married woman (Fanny Van de Grift Osbourne) and wouldn't become an engineer. He was nothing more substantial than a scribbler of words. And the character of Hyde, it seems to me, has a lot to do with the act of scribbling. Hyde is Stevenson's portrait of the artist as a bad little boy. His "littleness" helps identify his rage. Hyde has no imprint on this world other than his strange deformity. He's that unredeemed child in Jekyll (and Stevenson himself), that dwarf who stays asleep until Jekyll pushes him out and gives birth to Edward Hyde, his shrunken twin. But Hyde "escapes" from Jekyll, walks about London doing harm. Hyde is without civility. He tramples on people. He's that saddest of monsters, the artist who can find no shape to please him. He is energy coiled in upon itself, energy turned to hate.

2.

I can hear readers of *Dr. Jekyll and Mr. Hyde* scratch at me and shout: *How dare I intrude upon Robert Louis Stevenson's excellent horror story! Hyde is a fiend and nothing more, the worst of Jekyll, a monkey with corded hands. Hasn't the split between good and evil that Stevenson describes in the book become part of our general vocabulary? Jekyll and Hyde, the two faces that we wear. If we unloose the evil side of ourselves, as Jekyll does, it will bully the good, drive it under until evil is all—pure evil, that pale humpish creature called Hyde.* But Stevenson's art, his crafting of *Jekyll and Hyde,* acts against such neat interpretations of the story.

We should allow Jekyll to speak for himself. It's ironic that we stumble upon Jekyll's voice only after he's dead. We have his confession, his "full statement of the case," written for Gabriel John Utterson and presented to the reader. Jekyll's confession isn't quite so full as he would have his lawyer believe. Dr. Jekyll is that common literary pest, the unreliable narrator who tells us "everything," his wickedest thoughts, but whose earnestness is a form of evasion. Jekyll was born rich and "endowed besides with excellent parts." Earlier in the story, Utterson tells us that the good doctor "was wild when he was young." The nature of this wildness isn't revealed. Was he a whoremonger, a trampler of children (like Hyde himself), or a homosexual, as Nabokov suggests in his essay on Stevenson? Jekyll turns cold, becomes a scientific man, dabbles in metaphysics, and concludes that each of us is a "mere polity of multifarious, incongruous and independent denizens." And he dreams of separating out these different selves, the nasty ones and the good. He's willing to shake "the very fortress of identity" with the draught he prepares. He mixes the ingredients, watches them "boil and smoke together in the glass," and "with a strong glow of courage," he drinks the brew.

His agony begins, "a grinding in the bones, deadly nausea, and a horror of the spirit that cannot be exceeded at the hour of birth or death. Then these agonies began swiftly to subside, and I came to myself as if out of a great sickness. There was something strange in my sensations, something indescribably new and, from its very novelty, incredibly sweet. I felt younger, lighter, happier in body . . . I stretched out my hands, exulting in the freshness of these sensations; and in the act, I was suddenly aware that I had lost in stature."

The dwarf he becomes is Edward Hyde. When he looks at "that ugly idol" in the mirror, he's "conscious of no repugnance, rather of a leap of welcome. This, too, was myself. It seemed natural and human. In my eyes it bore a livelier image of the spirit, it seemed more express and single, than the imperfect and divided countenance I had been hitherto accustomed to call mine."

But the Jekyll in Hyde begins to grow anxious: "It yet remained to be seen if I had lost my identity beyond redemption and must flee before daylight from a house that was no longer mine." He drinks the brew and becomes Jekyll again.

And so he has the perfect life, two identities to play with, Jekyll and Hyde. He takes a house for Hyde in Soho and furnishes it. He thrills at the new power he has to become the smaller, younger Hyde whenever he desires. But something happens. He can no longer control these transformations, as Hyde begins to shove Jekyll out of the way. He would go to sleep as Henry Jekyll and wake as Edward Hyde. We find him "raging and freezing with the passions of Hyde."

"Hunted, houseless," he kills himself, and thus destroys Hyde, the monkey man. Virtue wins, and we have a completed history, if you trust Jekyll's account.

If Hyde is pure evil, sprung from Jekyll, why should he have been so puny? Jekyll explains this away with the notion that the evil side of him was "less robust and less developed" than the good; it was the weaker twin, held in check by the doctor's devotion to science and his abandoning of pleasure. But how "scientific" is Jekyll's search for Hyde? Isn't it more of an attempt to relieve a narrowed life that is intolerable now that he is fifty years old and has nothing but his own "decline" in front of him? Becoming Hyde, he feels "younger, lighter, happier in body." He welcomes Hyde's face in the mirror, that face we never see. He's in touch with a more primitive energy, perhaps his own sexual power that he's given up, the monkeylike side of him that a good Victorian such as Jekyll would have to interpret as evil. Hyde is "a murderous mixture of timidity and boldness," according to Utterson. And it is this mixture that counts. It suggests the hold that *Jekyll and Hyde* has had on readers since it appeared in 1886. Hyde is a timid monster, who is more child than killer man.

Hyde's murderousness may very well be the Jekyll
he carries around with him. He's as split as· the
doctor himself. He attempts to warn his Jekyll side,
the aging comfortable bachelor scientist, though Jekyll
sees this as "ape-like tricks." Hyde destroys the letters and portrait of Jekyll's father—a loaded trick, it
seems to me. There's a bit of Stevenson in this act,
Stevenson's own Jekyll warning him to escape the
cold industry of his father, that successful engineer.
Hyde scribbles "blasphemies" on the pages of Jekyll's
books, in Jekyll's own hand. This sense of signature
is quite important to the story. Jekyll opens a bank
account for his "twin," constructing Hyde's signature
with a backward "slope" of his own hand, so that
Hyde becomes Jekyll in reverse. But the monster
won't use this sly signature. No matter how deformed
he is, he writes with Jekyll's "hand."

3.

Dr. Jekyll and Mr. Hyde is a book of mirrors and
reversals. Jekyll conjures Hyde, falls in love with
that "ugly idól," and then flees from it. And thus we
have the apparent conflict of the story. Once Hyde is
out of the bottle, Jekyll can summon no magic to get
rid of him. Transmogrified into a monkey man, he
moans and dies. But the story doesn't end here.
Embedded in Jekyll's narrative is the world according to Hyde. The monster has no pages to list his

grievances and his groans. But the grievances are present if we choose to look.

It's never made clear why the monster tramples on the "aged beautiful gentleman," Sir Danvers Carew. The details are "few and startling." A maid-servant is sitting at her window in a "dream of musing," when she sees the older man accost the shrunken Hyde. The maid continues to observe from her window: "The moon shone on his [Sir Danvers's] face as he spoke . . . it seemed to breathe such an innocent and old-world kindness of disposition, yet with something high too, as of a well-founded self-content." Hyde doesn't answer the old man. He clutches his heavy cane, "and then all of a sudden he broke out in a great flame of anger, stamping with his foot, brandishing the cane, and carrying on (as the maid described it) like a madman. The old gentleman took a step back, with the air of one very much surprised and a trifle hurt; and at that Mr. Hyde broke out of all bounds and clubbed him to the earth. And next moment, with ape-like fury, he was trampling his victim under foot and hailing down a storm of blows, under which the bones were audibly shattered and the body jumped upon the roadway."

An act of random, meaningless violence until we discover on the next page that Sir Danvers was carrying a sealed envelope addressed to Gabriel John Utterson, and the violence doesn't seem so random at all. The lawyer is Hyde's enemy, sworn to seek out the monster and uncover who he is. Had Sir Danvers lost his way, as the maid suggests, and asked Hyde how to get to Utterson's place on Gaunt Street? And did Hyde boil at the mention of Utterson's name?

What about the maid herself? She is the one female "character" in a book devoted to bachelor men. "Romantically given," it's natural that she should prefer the beautiful Sir Danvers to the shrunken Hyde. Sir Danvers has no danger about him. She sees him as kind and "innocent," whereas the monster is sexually perverse, someone she'd have to fear. And in this world without women that the maid views from her window, isn't it possible that the kind old man is attempting to "proposition" Hyde, and that Hyde trampled him out of rage? We'll never know.

Is there a simpler explanation? Was Hyde raging at the stranglehold of respectability that Sir Danvers represents? Or was that twin inside him, Dr. Jekyll, ashamed of meeting Sir Danvers in Hyde's body and frightened of the "virtue" he's lost? The split in Jekyll is documented throughout the story, but it is the ambiguity of Hyde that is much nearer to Stevenson's enchantment over us. Like Bartleby the scrivener, Stevenson's monster is that haunted, divided creature whose energy is "uncivilized." He's the hunted child who has to depend on his "respectable" brother. Jekyll pays the bills. Hyde is the creator/destroyer who has been housed so long in Jekyll's body, he can find no locus for his energy. A pale incubus, he struggles against Jekyll and can do nothing but howl.

The power of *Jekyll and Hyde* is that it resists simple allegory. Good and evil shift from face to face, and Stevenson wears all of them in the story. Isn't he Hyde's secret sharer? Sickly and rebellious, he destroys his father's "portrait" by becoming an artist rather than an engineer. *Dr. Jekyll and Mr. Hyde* was written under the fever of a man trying to declare his own identity, and I can't help but think that part of Hyde was that pale scribbler in Stevenson, screaming to come out, a "murderous mixture of timidity and boldness" that all good writing is about.

Biographical Data

1850	born on November 13, Robert Lewis Balfour Stevenson (Robert Louis), at 8 Howard Place, Edinburgh, Scotland.
1853	moved to 17 Heriot Row in the same city.
1857	learned to read, somewhat belatedly.
1860	entered Edinburgh Academy.
1863	traveled in Europe with his family.
1866	enrolled in the University of Edinburgh as a student of engineering.
1870-71	wrote paper on lighthouses awarded silver medal by Royal Scottish Society of Arts.
1871-2	wrote for the undergraduate *Edinburgh University Magazine*.
1873	to London where he meets various literary celebrities. Another visit to Europe, to France and the Côte d'Azur.
1875	passed the Scottish bar and became a lawyer, but virtually abandoned practice before he began.
1876-8	met Fanny Van de Grift Osbourne in Grez, France, after a canoe trip through Belgium and France. Fell in love with her. Spent most of his time in France.
1879	followed Fanny to America on the "emigrant ship" *Devonia*.
1880	married Fanny in San Francisco.
1881-2	went to Davos, Switzerland, for treatment of tuberculosis.
1883-4	convalescence at Hyères on the French Riviera.
1884-7	living at Bournemouth, England, at his house Skerryvore.

1887   went to the United States, treated for tuberculosis at Saranac, New York.

1888   cruise to the South Seas on the yacht *Casco*.

1889   residence in Honolulu, Hawaii.

1890   settled in Samoa, near Apia, and built a house called Vailima, or the "five waters," after the five streams on the mountain where his house was set.

1894   died on December 3 of a cerebral hemorrhage. Buried there on Mt. Vaea under a tombstone engraved with an inscription from his poem, "Requiem":

Here he lies where he longed to be;
Home is the sailor, home from the sea,
And the hunter home from the hill.